ACTING OUT

Atheneum Books for Young Readers
NEW YORK   LONDON   TORONTO   SYDNEY

presents . . .

ACTING OUT

SIX ONE-ACT PLAYS! ☆ SIX NEWBERY STARS!

WITHDRAWN

featuring the playwrights:

AVI   SUSAN COOPER
SHARON CREECH   PATRICIA MacLACHLAN
KATHERINE PATERSON   RICHARD PECK

edited by **JUSTIN CHANDA**

ATHENEUM BOOKS FOR YOUNG READERS
An imprint of Simon & Schuster Children's Publishing Division
1230 Avenue of the Americas, New York, New York 10020
This book is a work of fiction. Any references to historical events,
real people, or real locales are used fictitiously. Other names, characters,
places, and incidents are products of the author's imagination, and
any resemblance to actual events or locales or persons,
living or dead, is entirely coincidental.

Book design by Mike Rosamilia
The text for this book is set in Fairfield Medium.
Manufactured in the United States of America
0210 FFG
4 6 8 10 9 7 5
Library of Congress Cataloging-in-Publication Data
Acting out / the playwrights, Avi . . . [et al.].
p.   cm.
ISBN-13: 978-1-4169-3848-4 (alk. paper)
ISBN-10: 1-4169-3848-6 (alk. paper)
1. Children's plays, American. I. Avi, 1937–
PS625.5.A37 2008
812'.60809282—dc22   2007023613

Performance Rights

CONTENTS

ACTING OUT

INTRODUCTION

If you're like me and believe there's a lot of truth to the saying "all the world's a stage," then this really is the book for you.

Six of the best-loved Newbery-winning authors have teamed up to bring you six original one-act plays, all in one book. It's a star-studded cast, to say the least. So why would Avi, Susan Cooper, Sharon Creech, Patricia MacLachlan, Katherine Paterson, and Richard Peck decide to write plays? Simple:

Because plays make for great reading. Reading a play is just like reading your favorite novel or short story, only you'll find a lot fewer quotation marks. Stage directions replace paragraphs, and the story unfolds through dialogue. Keep reading and before you know it, the characters' voices will become so clear you can actually hear what they sound like and imagine what they look like as they act out their scenes. Every play has its own rhythm, and once you get swept up in it, it's as if the theater has darkened and the lights have come up on a show that is running just for you.

Because plays are great for reading ALOUD. Whether you read all the parts yourself or you assign roles to your friends, once you start hearing lines out loud, the characters will become that much more real. Does this character have an accent? Does that one TALK VERY LOUDLY? Does another character *talksuperfastallthetime*? Inflections, pitch, tone—it all becomes important because *how* somebody says something tells you a lot about *why* they are saying it. And that *why* tells us about *who* they are. The best part? You and your cast of readers get to make all the decisions and interpretations. Read these plays one way, and suddenly jokes will become funnier. Read them another way, and the pauses are more meaningful, silence might just become dramatic. The point is, when you read plays aloud, they aren't just stories anymore. You'll start to hear living, breathing people engaged in all kinds of drama.

Because plays are great for ACTING OUT! In your room, in your backyard, or in your classroom, get these plays "on their feet." Act them out to see what happens. You can make the sets as elaborate or as simple as you want. You can use actual props or imaginary ones. However large or small your production is, you and your fellow cast members will not just be reading, you will be transported into the middle of the action. While you are in the world of the play, you can become a whole different person—thinking their thoughts, feeling their feelings, and saying their words. Just imagine—With this book alone, you can become Edgar Allen Poe at age twelve, a decrepit billionaire, a bewitched school teacher, a dancing delinquent, an invisible gnome, an ancient talking boulder (no kidding), or any number of other characters. Girls can play boy characters. Boys can play girls.

You can play someone five times your age.

You can even play the dog.

It's all up to you. And the next time you act out one of the plays, you can be someone else entirely.

When I asked these six authors to become six playwrights, I wanted them to be completely uninhibited. They were allowed to write a play about whatever they wanted, set it wherever and whenever they wanted, and have it feature whoever popped into their brains. There was only one rule that would tie all the plays together. It came from an improvisation game that's played in acting classes. The game is simple. Before actors begin an improvised scene, they each have to choose one random word. Every actor has to then say each of those words at least once during the scene. The words can come at any time and can be used in any way the actors like. It makes for some surprising and curious improvisations!

For this collection of one acts, there were six playwrights and six plays to be written. Stealing the rule from the improvisation game, I asked each playwright to choose one word. It could have been a favorite word, a goofy word, or even a word they thought might stump the other playwrights. They were allowed to use the words in any way they wanted, but each of the six words had to appear somewhere in their script.

What are the words they chose?

"Dollop," "hoodwink," "Justin," "knuckleball," "panhandle," and "raven."

How are they used?

Part of the fun of reading the plays will be finding out!

—Justin Chanda, editor

THE
BAD ROOM

by PATRICIA MacLACHLAN

CHARACTERS

JAKE .... A boy
KNUCKLEBALL .... Jake's dog
BELLA .... An excitable girl
RIFF .... A creative boy
ROLLIE .... A happy-go-lucky boy
MINNIE .... A shy, reclusive girl
MAURICE .... A talky, know-it-all boy
MR. BARNACLE .... Principal, age thirty-five
GRACE BRIM .... A beautiful, flashy young
                                          woman; age thirty

SCENE 1

Lights up. Stage center is a door marked PRINCIPAL, *a bench on either side of the door. A bored-looking boy,* JAKE, *sits on one bench, his dog at his feet. He yawns.*

The door opens and a hand points to the bench, and a well-dressed girl, BELLA, *comes out. She is obviously distressed and unused to being disciplined. She sits on the bench opposite the boy and bursts into tears.* JAKE *does not look up, but the dog goes over to her.*

BELLA (*shrinking back*): Yuck!
JAKE: That's not his name.
BELLA: I *know* that! (BELLA *sniffles for a while as the dog stares at her. Then she winds down.*)
BELLA: What IS his name?
JAKE: Knuckleball.
BELLA: That's a baseball pitch.

   (JAKE *looks up, surprised.*)

JAKE (*impressed*): It is.
BELLA: I have a cat named Dollop.

   (JAKE *doesn't say anything.*)

BELLA: That's a dumb name too. (BELLA *sniffs a bit more.*)

JAKE: Your first time in detention, isn't it?

(BELLA *nods, and after a moment she reaches out to stroke* KNUCKLEBALL. *The door opens, and* RIFF, *a boy in a leather jacket—obviously trying to dress older and tougher than he is—enters. He clumps into the room. He sits next to* BELLA, *and she slides down the bench away from him.*)

RIFF: Hey, Knuckleball! You get Jake in trouble again? (RIFF *looks sideways at* BELLA.) Hullo. What did you do, Bella? Comb your hair the wrong way in class?

JAKE: Go easy, Riff. It's her first time in detention.

RIFF: Ha! You'll get used to it. You'll get used to sitting in the BAAAD room with the rest of us. . . .

BELLA: You dress like a stereotype. That's a vocabulary word. And you're *vindictive.* You're the meanest boy in school!

(RIFF *stares at her for a moment, then gets up and goes over to sit next to* JAKE.)

RIFF: Yeah. That's me, all right. The meanest boy you know. (*He pats his knee, and* KNUCKLEBALL *goes over and sits happily by* RIFF. *Very softly.*) But Knuckleball doesn't know that. Do you?

BELLA (*deciding to answer* RIFF'*s earlier question*): I called Leelee Potts a miscreant. It made her cry, and I got thrown out of class. (BELLA *looks sideways at* RIFF.) That's a vocabulary word too.

RIFF: I know that. (*He leans down and stares into* KNUCKLEBALL's *eyes.*) I think Bella is a bit of a miscreant too. Don't you think?

BELLA (*protesting*): No!

RIFF (*still talking to* KNUCKLEBALL, *who loves the attention*): With a little "hypocrite" thrown in.

(BELLA *begins to cry again.* RIFF *rolls his eyes and continues to pet* KNUCKLEBALL. *The door opens again and* ROLLIE, *a smiling boy who doesn't seem to mind being there, comes in. He happily sits next to* RIFF.)

RIFF: What happened this time?

ROLLIE: I forgot my homework.

JAKE: Forgot it at home?

ROLLIE: No. Forgot to do it.

(RIFF *smiles.*)

ROLLIE (*to* RIFF): Why are you here?

RIFF: I'm annoying. (*He looks over at* BELLA.) And mean.

(MINNIE, *a nervous-looking girl, comes in and looks around to see who is there, then sits away from everyone and ignores them all.*)

RIFF (*sarcastically*): The talker is here.

(MAURICE *follows* MINNIE. *He wears glasses and carries a laptop.*)

MAURICE (*calling back through the open door*): This is not fair, you know. The constitution gives me rights. MANY rights. One is the pursuit of my happiness . . .

(*A teacher,* MR. BARNACLE, *comes in, carrying a clipboard.* MAURICE *opens his mouth to protest.*)

MAURICE: . . . and . . .

MR. BARNACLE (*holding up his hand to silence* MAURICE *as he stares at his clipboard*): Hush, Maurice. I have a right to MY happiness, too. (*He looks over then to see* KNUCKLEBALL.) Again, Jake?

JAKE: He loves me.

MR. BARNACLE (*resigned*): Yes. He does. But the law says he cannot be in a regular classroom. Okay, everyone. Two and a half days of in-school suspension, starting today. Don't forget your lunch the next two days. (*He beckons them all to follow.*)

MAURICE: I still think this is unfair . . . at least to me. It is unfair because . . .

(RIFF gets up and takes *MAURICE* by the arm, quieting him. *RIFF* takes a tissue out of his pocket and hands it to *BELLA* without looking at her. They all go out the door. The door closes, leaving *KNUCKLEBALL* inside. The door opens again and *JAKE* looks at *KNUCKLEBALL*. *KNUCKLEBALL* follows *JAKE* out the door, and the door closes.)

Blackout.

SCENE 2

The stage set revolves to the other side, where there is a dismal classroom: plain, no pictures on the walls and no decoration. Desks are scattered around. Everyone files in and takes a seat, MINNIE the farthest away. RIFF goes over to the blackboard and writes "THE BAD ROOM" in large letters. MR. BARNACLE enters.

RIFF: What fascinating thing will we do today? Write our life histories? (*He looks at BELLA.*) My life as a MIS-CREANT!?

MR. BARNACLE (*sighing*): You wouldn't be here at all if you . . . (*and he looks at each one as he begins to run down the list*) you didn't talk so much in class, Maurice, you didn't annoy the teacher, Riff—

ROLLIE: If I did my homework?

RIFF: And if Bella didn't toss around her vocabulary words.

MR. BARNACLE (*looking at MINNIE*): All you need to do, Minnie, is answer the questions the teacher asks you. That's all!

(MINNIE *folds her arms and stares straight ahead.* MR. BARNACLE *turns to* JAKE. *But before he can say anything,* JAKE *shakes his head and puts his arms around* KNUCKLEBALL. MR. BARNACLE *smiles a bit.*)

MR. BARNACLE: Today will be something new.

JAKE: Something new?

ROLLIE: What do you mean, "new"?

(MR. BARNACLE *smiles happily.*)

MR. BARNACLE: New. You bet. Have fun!

(MR. BARNACLE *exits. There is silence in the "bad room."*)

ROLLIE: Fun? What do you think he means?

(JAKE *shakes his head.*)

RIFF: What could be new or fun about detention? In the BAD room?
JAKE: It's always boring here.
ROLLIE: Knuckleball likes it!
JAKE (*smiling*): *Knuckleball* likes everything!

(*The door opens and* MS. BRIM *enters. She is beautiful, startlingly dressed in rather flashy clothes. She carries a portable CD player.*)

MS. BRIM: Well, now here's an interesting array of faces!

(*Everyone is speechless.* JAKE's *jaw drops at the sight of her,* ROLLIE *stares,* MAURICE *shuts his laptop,* BELLA *smiles a bit.* MINNIE *stares.* KNUCKLEBALL *walks over to greet her.* MS. BRIM *pets* KNUCKLEBALL.)

MS. BRIM: Sit.

(KNUCKLEBALL *sits.*)

JAKE (*stunned*): He never sits on command. Never.

RIFF (*aside to the others*): This does not look boring.

(MS. BRIM *looks around and notices "THE BAD ROOM" written on the blackboard.*)

MS. BRIM: Ah, the bad room. I'm in the right place! (*She puts down the CD player.*) My name is Grace Brim. Ms. Brim. I have volunteered to take over the bad room.

(RIFF *turns so that* MS. BRIM *can't see him and grins widely at the others.* MS. BRIM *sits down in a chair and folds her arms as if waiting for something. There is silence, and finally* MAURICE *speaks.*)

MAURICE: Why? Why would you want to volunteer in this place? This is the "bad room." We have defined this as the "bad room," and therefore we are all "bad" here.

MS. BRIM (*smiling*): What is your name? (*She looks at a sheet of paper to find a name.*)

MAURICE: My name is Maurice. Maurice Hector Willoughby Trapp.

MS. BRIM: I think I'll just call you Maurice. The truth is I know all about the bad room. When I was your age, I spent lots of time in the bad room, though we called it something much worse.

(MS. BRIM *folds her arms again and waits.*)

ROLLIE: What did *you* call it? (*Beat.*) I'm Rollie.

MS. BRIM: We called it "the dumb room," Rollie. And that was worse. Much, much worse.

BELLA: That's awful!

MAURICE: It's revolting . . . not kind at all. And furthermore . . .

ROLLIE (*interrupting softly*): Sometimes they call me dumb.

(*Everyone turns to look at ROLLIE.*)

MS. BRIM: Well, that IS cruel. And no one in our bad room was dumb or cruel. We weren't bad, either. (*She looks over at the blackboard.*) In fact (*she stands up and looks around the room at everyone*), we were smart and kind. And here is the big secret: We were the best!

(*ROLLIE grins. The others giggle. KNUCKLEBALL gets excited.*)

RIFF: So, why did you get sent to the . . . (*There's a beat as he tries to decide what to call the room.*) . . . the bad room.

MS. BRIM (*looking at a paper list*): Are you Richard?

(*Everyone laughs.*)

RIFF (*looking warningly at the others*): I'm Riff.

MS. BRIM: I won't forget that, Riff. I forgot to do my homework; sometimes I was bored in class. . . . I fell asleep. . . . Talked too much, didn't talk at all. There were lots of things.

JAKE: You WERE bad!

(There is laughter again.)

MS. BRIM: Not really bad. . . . I was shy and needed to be good at something. And . . . that's what we're going to do here. We're going to learn something new and be really good at it! Everyone else in the whole school will wish they could do it as well as we do. The truth of it is, if you can do one thing well, you can do many other things well, too.

MAURICE: What? What will that be? I'm already good at talking and many other things . . . including—

RIFF (*interrupting*): We know what you're good at, Maurice Hector Willoughby Trapp.

(MS. BRIM goes over to the blackboard and crosses out "THE BAD ROOM." She writes "THE BALL-ROOM" in large letters. She presses the play button on her CD recorder. Loud waltz music fills the room. RIFF, JAKE, MINNIE, ROLLIE, BELLA, and MAURICE look at one another, mystified as the music goes on. After a while, MS. BRIM turns off the music)

BELLA: What was that?

MAURICE: That is my grandma's music. Sometimes she and my grandfather play music.

MS. BRIM: That is the waltz! Do any of you know how to waltz?

(They all shake their heads.)

MS. BRIM: Can you dance at all?

(They nod their heads. MS. BRIM smiles.)

MS. BRIM: Show me!

(Everyone looks uncomfortable. They squirm. MS. BRIM puts a new CD in the player. It is more familiar music to them all.)

MS. BRIM *(firmly):*   Show me now!

(One by one, they get up and begin to dance. ROLLIE bounces, MAURICE does a strange hunched-over dance, MINNIE moves from side to side, JAKE and BELLA dance next to each other. RIFF starts to dance with KNUCKLEBALL, and KNUCKLEBALL begins to bark. Everyone laughs.)

MS. BRIM *(calling):* Good! You're moving! Tomorrow we're all going to learn how to waltz! And maybe . . . just maybe we'll go on to the cha-cha, and meringue. . . .

(Everyone stops and moves back to their desks.)

RIFF: Oh, no. I don't think so.
MAURICE: I don't want to. Dancing is not one of the things I think I want to do, actually. Perhaps another time.

MS. BRIM (*slowly*): Well, there is an alternative. . . .
JAKE: What?

(MS. BRIM *begins handing out papers, walking from one desk to another.*)

MS. BRIM: We can write some essays . . . and I have here somewhere some *very interesting* (*she says that slowly and slyly*) math problems, and I think some other homework . . . and some vocabulary words to use in sentences: hoodwink, panhandle . . . and . . .
MAURICE (*interrupting*): Oh, oh! I know panhandle! It means an elongated peninsula-type formation with land on one side or . . .
RIFF: Okay, okay.
JAKE: We'll dance.
MS. BRIM (*brightly*): Riff says okay. Jake says yes. What about the rest of you? Who here will be delighted and excited to learn ballroom dancing?

(MS. BRIM *looks around and waits. Slowly, all the hands go up, one after the other.*)

MS. BRIM: We're going to *wow* ourselves with our dancing! And then we're going to *wow* everyone else!
ROLLIE (*as if he likes the word*): Wow!

Blackout.

SCENE 3

Lights up on the next day in the "bad room." JAKE and KNUCKLEBALL are the only ones there, sitting at the edge of the stage. JAKE pets KNUCKLEBALL. MINNIE enters and stops when she sees JAKE and KNUCKLEBALL. She is wearing a bright sweater and has combed her hair neatly. As if making a decision that isn't easy, she comes over to sit next to JAKE.

MINNIE: Jake?

(*JAKE looks up, surprised that it is MINNIE talking to him. Behind him MS. BRIM enters quietly and puts her CD player on the table. Neither MINNIE nor JAKE notices her. MS. BRIM sees them talking and is quiet so as not to bother them.*)

MINNIE: When I walked to school today, I saw you.

(*JAKE looks down at KNUCKLEBALL as if he knows what MINNIE is about to say.*)

MINNIE: Knuckleball wasn't following you. He was on a leash.

(*JAKE doesn't say anything.*)

MINNIE: He doesn't follow you to school, does he?

(*JAKE shakes his head and pets KNUCKLEBALL.*)

JAKE: I have to live with my grandmother. She gets asthma from Knuckleball.

(MINNIE *reaches out to pet* KNUCKLEBALL.)

JAKE: I keep him in my room when I'm home. Away from Grandma. She can't help it, you know. She likes him. But I have to bring him to school. I *have* to.
MINNIE: I know. Maybe we can find a way . . .
JAKE: A way?
MINNIE: To help. I like Knuckleball. He doesn't care if I don't talk. Knuckleball doesn't care. Sometimes it isn't easy for me to find the right things to say.

(JAKE *smiles.*)

JAKE: But you just did, Minnie. You said the right thing.
MINNIE: Our secret?
JAKE: Our secret.

(MS. BRIM *doesn't say anything, but she has heard the conversation. And then the rest come into the room. They settle into their desk seats nervously, as* MS. BRIM *tapes some pictures of dancers up on the wall. She turns around.*)

MS. BRIM: Dancing is a way to speak without words. Remember that when you dance, you are part of a story. YOUR story.
ROLLIE: What kind of story?

(MS. BRIM *shrugs her shoulders and smiles.*)

MS. BRIM: That's why you dance. To find out the story. And to find out who you are.

(MS. BRIM *beckons them all to stand up.*)

MS. BRIM: Stand behind me in a line. And follow me. This will be one, two, three; one, two, three; one, two, three. Later we'll do partners. Okay?
RIFF (*grinning*): Okay.

(MS. BRIM *starts the music, a Viennese waltz. Everyone lines up behind* MS. BRIM. MS. BRIM *begins to move in a waltz, all of them watching and following behind.* ROLLIE *laughs,* MINNIE *grins and they continue to follow* MS. BRIM *as music fills the room. They don't see* MR. BARNACLE *open the door and look inside, watching them begin to learn the waltz. Slowly, he closes the door.*)

Blackout.

SCENE 4
Lights up the next day in the "bad room," which is full of laughter. RIFF *is there without his leather jacket, looking a bit more like the others. Everyone clears up the lunch clutter.*

MS. BRIM: All right, dancers! You've mastered the step. Now we do partners.

MAURICE (*clapping his hands to his face in horror*): Partners? Oh, no . . .

ROLLIE: Who is my partner?

BELLA: Don't worry, Rollie. You aren't the gray wolf. You don't have a partner for life.

MS. BRIM (*laughing*): We'll change partners, Rollie. Lets see . . . four boys, two girls. Some boy has to be a girl.

RIFF: I'll be a girl!

(*Everyone laughs.*)

RIFF: I can dance backward.

MINNIE (*indignant*): Hey, why SHOULD girls have to dance backward?

RIFF: She speaks!

JAKE: She does.

MS. BRIM: Don't worry. Soon you'll be whirling and dipping around so you won't even feel like you're going backward.

ROLLIE (*alarmed*): Dipping?

MS. BRIM: Rollie, you dance with Riff. (*Everyone giggles.*) Jake and Minnie. Maurice and Bella. A hand on your partner's waist . . . like this. (MS. BRIM *goes around and places their hands on their partner's waists*). Hands out, heads up. You're proud, remember.

RIFF: Yeah.

BELLA (*worried*): I've never whirled or dipped before.

JAKE: You'll be okay. Any girl who knows what a knuckleball is will be okay.

(MS. BRIM *turns on the music.*)

MS. BRIM: Dance to the music, remember!

(They begin dancing, moving around the room.)

MS. BRIM: Listen to the music. Fly, Minnie. Soar like an eagle! Fly like a raven!

(They all dance, moving with more confidence now. After a bit the song ends.)

MS. BRIM: Now, that was wonderful!
BELLA: Really? Wonderful?
MAURICE: Not perfect.

(MS. BRIM laughs.)

MS. BRIM: Perfect takes a while.
ROLLIE *(rather sadly)*: And detention is over. . . . We've run out of time.
JAKE *(thoughtfully)*: Maybe . . .

(He stops, embarrassed, and everyone looks at him.)

RIFF: Maybe what?
JAKE: Maybe we could practice after school. For a while.
MS. BRIM: Come to the "bad room"? After school?
RIFF: It's not the "bad room" anymore. It's the ballroom.

(MS. BRIM smiles broadly.)

MS. BRIM: That it is! And maybe you could have a recital—a performance on Friday night.

BELLA: Just for us. A dance just for us.

JAKE: And Knuckleball.

MS. BRIM: You'd better keep practicing for Knuckleball!

(MS. BRIM *turns the music back on.*)

MS. BRIM (*over the music*): Once again now. Heads up! Fly like a bird, Minnie. . . .

(*Everyone dances. The door opens again and several children peer in. More come to look. As RIFF passes the door, he pushes it shut so they can't see anymore.*)

Blackout.

SCENE 5

Lights up. It is Friday. The "bad room" has become the "ballroom." There are lights strung around the room, and crepe-paper decorations everywhere, crisscrossing the room and dipping from the ceiling. The room has been transformed: no desks anymore; even more pictures on the walls. A refreshment table stands at one end, covered with a white tablecloth. There are glasses and a punch bowl. Suddenly, there is a loud commotion outside the room. The door opens, and we can see lots of children out in the hallway. Then MS. BRIM enters, dressed in a long gown, her hair piled on top of her head.

Behind her are ROLLIE, MAURICE, JAKE, *and* RIFF *dressed in suits, their hair slicked down.* MINNIE *and* BELLA *come in, wearing beautiful long dresses.* MINNIE *has feathers in her hair.* ROLLIE *sits down quickly and takes out a book, paper, and pencil. He writes frantically.*

RIFF (*calling to the crowd outside*): Sorry! This is *our* party!

(*He closes the door.*)

JAKE: Wait!

(JAKE *hurries to the door and opens it.* KNUCKLEBALL *comes in, a satin ribbon tied around his neck.*)

MINNIE: Rollie? What are you doing?
ROLLIE (*not looking up*): Finishing my homework . . . almost . . . done!

(ROLLIE *closes his book with a slap and leaps up.*)

MS. BRIM: Well! Look at you all! You're beautiful. And I hope you've had fun. (*She pauses.*) Not sure if you learned much, or if you got your homework done.
ROLLIE: I did mine! Last night, too!
BELLA: And Minnie talks a lot more.
RIFF (*grinning*): Maurice doesn't.

(Everyone turns to look at MAURICE. *He smiles and tilts his head.)*

MAURICE: Not all the time.

BELLA: I learned Riff isn't the meanest boy in school.

RIFF: Still annoying, though.

JAKE: Mr. Barnacle told me Knuckleball could come to school and stay in the bad room whenever he wanted.

MS. BRIM: The ballroom, you mean.

JAKE (*to* MS. BRIM): Did you speak to Mr. Barnacle about Knuckleball?

*(MS. BRIM *shakes her head.*)*

MS. BRIM: I think that was *your* secret. It must have been someone else.

*(JAKE *looks at* MINNIE. *She smiles.*)*

JAKE (*amazed*): You?

MINNIE: It wasn't hard to talk to Mr. Barnacle.

BELLA (*rather sadly*): I'll miss this room.

RIFF: Don't worry. Some of us will be back.

JAKE: Knuckleball will!

BELLA (*speaks haltingly and shyly*): Maybe . . . maybe we could . . . somehow . . . keep going.

JAKE: Keep going?

MINNIE: You mean dancing?

RIFF: Why not? I haven't mastered dipping yet.

JAKE: And there's the cha-cha.

(RIFF *turns to* MS. BRIM.)

RIFF: Would you keep teaching us?
(MS. BRIM *smiles.*)

MS. BRIM: I would. (*She turns on the music.*) Time for dancing!

(*Everyone begins to dance—if anything, dancing better in their beautiful costumes.*)

RIFF (*calling to* MS. BRIM): What about you?

(*Just in time, the door opens and MR. BARNACLE enters in his suit, carrying a bouquet of flowers. He presents them to MS. BRIM and they begin to dance too.*)

Lights fade to black.

Production Note for *The Bad Room*

As far as I can see, the main physical challenge is the first scene, with the benches by the principal's door revolving into the next scene, the Bad Room. This could be done with a platform on wheels, simply wheeling the principal's door and benches away to the next scene.

The other challenge is the dog, Knuckleball. You could, of course, use a person dressed in a dog costume to play Knuckleball. Even more interesting, you could use a dog who likes to be onstage and can actually sit on command. (My dogs, who do absolutely *nothing* I tell them most of the time, will sit when I ask.) Have fun.

—P. M.

THE
RAVEN

by SHARON CREECH

CHARACTERS

TRISH .... The editor, late twenties

EDGAR A. POE .... The author, age twelve

ASSISTANT .... Female, early twenties

B. D. .... The managing director, male, mid-forties

DELIVERY BOY .... Late teens

Lights up on a normal workday in an editor's office in New York City. The office is small, cramped, and in general disarray, with heaps of manuscripts on the furniture and floor. Bookcases on right side wall are stuffed with books and more manuscripts. In the center of the room is the editor's desk, with computer and telephone, jars filled with pencils and pens, piles of manuscripts, stacks of Post-it notes, and a large thesaurus. On the wall behind the editor's desk are two red lights and two green lights, which will flash during the scene as indicated. Also on this wall are dozens of Post-it notes, with hand-written reminders on them. At left is the door, open to the hallway. As the scene opens, TRISH, *the editor, is sitting behind the desk. She is in her late twenties, dressed young and hip, with wild, unkempt hair. She is looking at a slim manuscript on the desk before her. To the left side of* TRISH's *desk sits a boy, about twelve years of age: the author* EDGAR POE. *He is wearing an ill-fitting (too small) black suit, wrinkled white shirt, and dark tie. He appears sullen and reserved, morose. This is his first visit to an editor's office.*

TRISH (*looking up from manuscript*): I can't tell you how
  pleased we are to have you aboard (*checks manuscript*),
  Edgar Poe. So young! Twelve years old! And so talented!
POE: If you insist.

TRISH: We are tickled absolutely to death.

POE: I see.

TRISH: Ecstatic. Absolutely (*reaches for thesaurus, skims, continues*) gratified. Jubilant. Rapt!

POE: Rapt?

TRISH: Enchanted. Transported. Tickled. Thrilled! (TRISH *looks at* POE *expectantly.*)

(*Awkward pause.*)

POE: Ah. My turn? I am . . . pleased. (*As* TRISH *continues to stare at him,* POE *reluctantly forges on.*) Delighted. And thrilled. And (*grabs thesaurus, rapidly skimming pages*) perhaps hoodwinked—no, no, not hoodwinked, rather, instead, abashed, and (*struggling*) transported.

TRISH: Oh, goodness. Transported? Well done! (*Behind* TRISH, *single red light flashes on wall.*) Oh, no! (*Dials phone.*) Who? (*Gasps, hangs up, scribbles on Post-it note, attaches note to wall.*)

POE: What are those lights, Miss—?

TRISH: Trish. Just call me Trish. The lights? Single red light means our competition has made a discovery.

POE: Discovery?

TRISH: New author. An unknown. A genius!

POE (*skeptically*): A genius?

TRISH: Double red lights mean our competition has hit the bestseller list.

POE: Which is, I suppose, bad?

TRISH: Bad? It's terrible! Horrific! (*reaches for thesaurus, skims*) Atrocious! Revolting! Nauseating!

POE: And the green lights?

TRISH: Same thing, but for *us. Our* discoveries. *Our* best-sellers. We, of course, want to see those *green* lights flashing and *not* the red ones! Ha, ha. And speaking of discoveries, I can't tell you how very, very—

POE: Transported?

TRISH: Yes! How very, very *transported* we are that you are with us (*checks name on manuscript*), Edgar Poe. Eddie? May I call you Eddie?

POE: No. It's Edgar. Edgar Allan Poe, to be precise, and I prefer to be precise.

TRISH: I see. Precise. Now then, I quite enjoyed your manuscript (*reads title from manuscript*) "The Raven." And we are *very close*—very close—Eddie, to being able to make an offer.

POE: Edgar.

TRISH: Quite.

POE: I had hoped—I had thought—or rather . . . (POE *raises both arms theatrically.*) Was it hope? Thought? (*He taps his chin, stares at the ceiling.*) I was *speculating* that today you might make an offer—

TRISH: I get your drift, Eddie—and I do assure you that we are very, very close—we are almost (*checks thesaurus*), ah yes, *impending!*

POE: I hesitate to be too bold—

TRISH: Not to worry. Never fear. Don't bother yourself. Don't fret. We can be per-fect-ly honest here—
(*Phone rings.* TRISH *answers.*) Yes? Elaine? I'm with an AUTHOR at the moment— No! When? (TRISH *taps double red light. Double red light flashes.*) Rats!

(TRISH *hangs up phone, scribbles note, attaches note to wall. To* POE) Would you like coffee? Tea?

POE: Water? If it isn't too much trouble . . .

TRISH: Of course not. Water it is. (*Dials phone.*) Trish here. Two *agua.* Quickly, quickly. (*Hangs up.*)

(ASSISTANT *appears in doorway. She is young and groovy, chewing gum.*)

ASSISTANT: Fizzy or still?

TRISH: Eddie? Your preference?

POE: Pardon?

TRISH: Fizzy or still?

POE: I AM feeling sort of fizzy—

TRISH: No, no, you funny boy! Ha, ha. Do you want fizzy *water* or still *water?*

POE: Oh. (*stiffly*) Ha, ha. Fizzy, I guess.

TRISH (*reeling*): *Fizzy?*

POE: No, no, still! Yes, still. I'll have still water.

(ASSISTANT *exits.*)

TRISH: Now, let's get down to business. After all, that's what we're here for, yes? Business! As I mentioned, the offer, of course, is impending—

POE: Imminent? (*Proud of himself for thinking of this word.*)

TRISH: Oh, there's a word for you. Imminent. Yes, why not? Imminent, imminent. (*Scrawls word on paper, adds to wall.*) But first, of course, there are a few small matters I would like to discuss.

POE: Oh. I hope—or rather fear—

TRISH: Not to worry. Merely a few incidentals, a few trifles, a few dollops—

POE: *Dollops?*

TRISH: Yes. (TRISH *carefully restacks manuscript on her desk.*) Let's get down to the nitty-gritty with your manuscript, "The Raven." How very unique. Truly, truly unique. Wherever did you come up with this idea—the big and stately black bird? How clever, to call it a raven!

POE: It IS a raven.

TRISH: Truly? How fascinating. (*Single red light flashes.*) Oh! (*Dials phone.*) Trish here. Which publisher? Knopf? The discovery? No! A baker in Boston? Rats! (*Hangs up, makes note, attaches to wall. To* POE) Let's see now, where were—oh yes, your unique, um, manuscript. We do have a few minor questions regarding the—how shall I put it?—regarding the—well, we can be honest here, yes? The *title*! It is the title about which—

POE (*confused*): The title?

TRISH: Minor, minor questions. Not even questions. How shall I—perhaps merely little rumbles. No. Too strong! Entirely too strong! Little *tingles*, yes, *tingles* of concern. The title is so very important. Crucial! Think about it. It is absolutely vital to the selling strategy. You understand?

POE: I, uh—

TRISH: Of course, I would not object to your simple title—
oh, don't get me wrong—not "simple" as in "simple-
minded"! I mean simple as in, how shall I put it—
POE: Uncomplicated?
TRISH: Ah yes, uncomplicated. But we must be very careful
here. Very and totally aware of market trends, strategies,
selling points—

(B. D. *appears at doorway. He is the managing director,*
middle-aged, dressed in slacks, white shirt, and red tie.
While he talks with TRISH, POE *wanders over to book-*
case and runs his finger along the spines.)

B. D.: Sorry, not to interrupt, but it's "go" for the mil.
TRISH: That all, B. D.?
B. D.: 'Fraid so. Ciao.

(B. D. *exits.*)

TRISH (*dials phone*): Elaine? Trish here. Just had a word
with B. D., the MD, and we're prepared to offer one
million for Jack's latest. The one that reads, thus far,
"It was . . ." Yes, I realize that he expects more than
a mil. Okay, I'll try. Cheerio. Ciao. (*Hangs up. Dials.*)
B. D.? Need more. Righty-oh. (*Hangs up.*)

(DELIVERY BOY *enters with water, which he places on*
Trish's desk. He is in his late teens and wears jeans and a
blue shirt with his company's insignia—"We Deliver!"—

on the back. TRISH *pays* BOY *and* BOY *exits.* TRISH *adds note to wall and dials phone.*)

TRISH: Accounting? Trish here. Expenses. Author: two waters. No, one for author, one for me. Total of two. Forty-five dollars. Righty-oh. (*Hangs up. To* POE) Where were we?

POE (*turning from bookcase*): The title. (*He returns to his chair and sits.*)

TRISH: Ah yes, strategies, et cetera. The two-word title is OUT. Out, out, out!

POE: Out?

TRISH: Quite. Out. Your use of "The" is fine, mind you. Absolutely terrific! But we need "The something-something." You follow? (*As she continues, she stands and paces behind her desk.*) "The Raven Code," perhaps? "The Raven KNUCKLEBALL"? Or, better yet, "Something-something and the something-something." Let's say "Polly Raven and the Silver Chalice," mm?

POE (*mortified*): But there is no Polly, and no chalice—

TRISH (*still pacing behind desk*): Quite. I take your point. But to appeal to the widest audience, it should be easy to add a Polly and a silver chalice, mm? And perhaps, to jazz up the sympathy, maybe get a panhandler in there? You know, a poor beggar child sort of thing? Oh! And to bring in the male audience, some war or spies or baseball? "Polly Panhandler and the Baseball Chalice War"? Mm?

POE (*aghast, but trying to be cooperative*): But there's no war, no baseball—

TRISH (*sits at her desk*): Now, moving right along, there is the teeny tiny small matter of the opening. (TRISH *reads from manuscript.*) "Once upon a midnight dreary . . ."

POE (*smiling, obviously pleased with his opening line*): I worked *six months* on that one line.

TRISH: Oh, but of course you did. Of course. Listen again. (*This time, as* TRISH *reads, she makes the word "dreary" sound exceedingly dreary.*) "Once upon a midnight DREARY . . ."

POE: I don't quite get what—

TRISH: Hold on a sec. (TRISH *dials phone. On phone*) Can you come in here? Now. (*Hangs up phone. To* POE) Let's see if I can demonstrate—

(ASSISTANT *enters.*)

ASSISTANT: Yeah?

TRISH (*to* ASSISTANT): Listen to this. Give me your honest reaction, okay?

ASSISTANT: Okay.

TRISH (*reads from* POE's *manuscript. Again, she makes the word "dreary" sound exceedingly dreary.*): "Once upon a midnight *dreary* . . ."

ASSISTANT: Gosh. Sounds a little *dreary* to me.

TRISH: Pre-cise-ly!

ASSISTANT: I'd use something like (*waving hand in air as if fishing for a word*), like *sunny!*

(POE *visibly reels.*)

TRISH (*scornfully*): Pish, pish.

ASSISTANT: That all?

TRISH (*dismissively*): Yes.

(*ASSISTANT exits.*)

TRISH (*to* POE): There, you see? Quite dreary, that opening.

POE (*nodding*): Yes, exactly. That's what I was going for there: set the mood, the tone. Immediately you get the feeling—

TRISH (*dismayed*): You were *hoping* it would sound dreary?

POE: Sure, because the whole poem—

TRISH: Yes, yes, I know, the talking raven and all that, but you see, you cannot have such a dreary opening.

POE (*starting to shake*): I can't?

TRISH (*leans forward, making her point*): Absolutely a no-no! We don't want the readers all depressed right off the bat, do we? No, no, no. Why, they'll close that little book before they get to the second line. (*She leans back, satisfied that she has made her point.*)

POE: And you're suggesting—

TRISH: Of course, I don't want to write your book for you, but how about something along the lines of, hmm, let's see, how about: "Once upon a *sunny* morning . . ." There! How's that? Cheers the whole thing right up! Why, it makes me happy just thinking of it. A sunny morning, the birdies warbling, that sort of thing.

POE (*beginning to unravel*): The whole *point* is that the speaker is feeling so *dreary*, so depressed, so morose, if you will—and that's why the black raven—

TRISH: Yes, yes, I know, scary black ravens (*feigns fear, making a face and trembling*), such depressing birds, aren't they? But maybe if it's a sunny morning, he sees, oh, I don't know, maybe a bluebird? Oh, a bluebird! Mm?

POE (*choking*): A BLUEBIRD?

TRISH: Whatever. Bluebird, robin, chickadee. You'll think of something. Oh, and another point. Poetry. You do it quite well, absolutely, but poetry, I'm afraid, is *out* these days.

POE (*near tears*): But the whole manuscript is—

TRISH: Poetry! Exactly! You see the problem! If we make an offer—

POE: IF?

TRISH: A thousand pardons! *When* we make an offer. A slip of the tongue. When! Of course, absolutely! (*Single and double red lights flash. TRISH dials the phone.*) Rats. Hello? Who? When? Penguin? A butcher in Baltimore? Rats! (*Hangs up. Phone rings. TRISH answers.*) Yes? B. D.? Two million? That's all? Righty-oh. (*Hangs up. To POE*) Now where were—

POE (*weary now*): Poetry. Out.

TRISH: Absolutely! How perceptive you are for such a young lad. We would like to see this unique, unique manuscript rendered in prose.

(*Pause. POE is stunned, struggling to maintain his composure.*)

POE: Not poetry?

TRISH: Prose.

POE (*apparently defeated*): Prose.

TRISH: Do you think you can manage? Oh, and then there is the matter of length. I know I can be candid. I would not take the trouble if we did not have complete and total faith in your ability—

POE (*Flattery has worn thin on him now. He is dumbfounded, despairing but trying to control himself.*): Mm.

TRISH: It is the matter of length which needs, how shall I put it, the length needs, um, lengthening. Yes, that's it!

POE (*stiffly*): What sort of length did you have in mind?

TRISH: Let's see. (*Weighs manuscript in hand.*) How long is it now?

POE: Six pages.

TRISH: In words, I meant. That's the lingo. Fifty thousand? A hundred thousand?

POE: Four hundred twenty.

TRISH: Pardon?

POE: Four hundred twenty. There are four hundred twenty words in my poem.

TRISH: I say! Four hundred and twenty? Of course, when you turn it into prose, that will help. Adding all the *and*'s, *the*'s, et cetera. Four hundred and twenty words is just a bit, how shall I say—

POE (*clipped*): Short?

TRISH: Precisely! Exactly! You are entirely too perceptive. Shall we expand, mm?

POE: "We"?

TRISH: You. I mean you, of course. Do you think, is it feasible, say, for you to expand to, say, two hundred and fifty thousand?

POE: Words? Two hundred fifty thousand words? (*incredulous*) You mean you want me to add . . . (POE *reaches for notepad, scribbles, figuring.*) two hundred forty-nine thousand five hundred eighty words?

TRISH (*oblivious to POE's discomfort*): Brilliant! Could you? Feasible?

POE (*mortified. Stiffly*): It might take me a while.

(B. D. *rushes in.*)

B. D.: Sorry, not to interrupt, but flash! Takeover on horizon.

TRISH: No, B. D.! Who?

B. D.: P. G. by H. B.

TRISH (*relieved*): Whew! Not us!

B. D.: Keep you posted. Cheerio. Ta-ta.

(B. D. *exits.*)

TRISH: Now, where were—

POE (*resigned*): Length. Adding two hundred forty-nine thousand five hundred eighty words. Time. How long. Feasibility.

TRISH: Quite. What a pleasure to work with someone who understands. And you're so young! Let's see. How long do you think—?

POE: Two or three—

TRISH: Days? Magnificent!

POE: Actually, I was thinking, or hoping, or wishing, more along the lines of—

TRISH: Weeks?

POE: Er—

TRISH: Months? Years?

POE (*weakly*): Decades.

TRISH (*figuring, on paper*): Mm, two or three decades, mm. In terms of years, that is, mm, what would you say, somewhere in the neighborhood of, what, say, twenty or thirty years?

POE: If it would not be too presumpt—

TRISH: Not at all! The muse, the little gray cells, it all takes time, quite. I'll make a note—we may expect the finished manuscript in, what, say, two thousand twenty-eight?

POE: Or two thousand thirty-eight. Somewhere in there.

TRISH: Quite. (*Makes note.*) All set?

POE: Er, there was the little matter of the offer. The advance.

TRISH: Moolah! Absolutely!

(B. D. *rushes in, looks about nervously.*)

B. D.: I heard a rumor.

TRISH: No! What?

B. D.: Someone being fired. Axed. Terminated.

TRISH: No! Who? Me?

B. D.: No, me.

TRISH: No! Can't be true! Not to worry! Never fear!

B. D.: Truly?

TRISH: Truly. Trust me. Now, B. D., as long as you're here, I was just discussing with this AUTH-OR (*Reaches for manuscript, checks name.*) Poe. Edgar. Eddie. Very young. Quite. "The Raven."

(B. D. scowls)

TRISH: Not to worry. Discussed. Thinking more along the lines of "Polly Panhandler and the Baseball Chalice War."

B. D.: Brilliant! Length?

TRISH: At present? Four twenty.

B. D.: Tuh! Too—

TRISH: Yes, yes, too short, expanding, to two hundred and fifty thousand words. By what year? Two thousand twenty-eight.

POE (*weakly*): Or two thousand thirty-eight.

TRISH: Or two thousand thirty-eight. In that neighborhood.

B.D.: Rightie-oo. (*Jots down figures on paper, hands to* TRISH.)

TRISH: Brilliant! (*to* POE) I think we are making headway. I believe we can offer—

POE (*excited*): What, *now*?

TRISH: Precisely. How does five hundred sound?

POE (*ecstatic*): Five hundred thousand dollars?

TRISH: Er, five *hundred* dollars.

POE (*forlorn*): What? Five hundred dollars? (POE *snatches up his manuscript.*) For the poetry into prose (*tosses a page into the air*), for the changing of the . . . (*tosses another page into the air*), for the adding of the . . . (*tosses another page*) for the days, weeks, months, years, decades . . . (POE *tosses remaining pages into the air.*)

TRISH: I sense some dis-ap-point-ment. But this is our standard offer for a first work. You must keep in mind that it is merely an advance. You will earn royalties on whatever you sell above and beyond—

POE: Oh. How many copies will you print?

TRISH: For a first book? Somewhere in the neighborhood of, say, twenty-two.

POE (*unglued*): TWENTY-TWO? But then how could I earn royalties on—

(B. D. *whispers to* TRISH.)

TRISH: Oh, and B. D. suggests we change your name.

POE (*stunned*): My *name*?

TRISH: Market strategies, sales promo, all that, you understand? Edgar Poe is just not, how shall I phrase it, not quite *right*. That's it. Not quite right.

POE (*barely able to speak*): And what sort of—

TRISH: Along the lines of—let's take first names first, mm? You need initials, jazzy ones, like, say, J. Z. Or something zingy, like, say, Avocado. And last names, two syllables, absolutely. Bowling? Pickett?

(*Red lights flash frantically.* B. D. *snatches phone, dials.*)

B. D. (*on phone*): What? No!

(ASSISTANT *rushes in.*)

ASSISTANT (*waving papers at* TRISH): What does this say? One million dollars or two million dollars?

(DELIVERY BOY *enters.*)

DELIVERY BOY: Hey, I—

POE (*thinking aloud*): Five hundred dollars is hardly enough to—

B. D. (*on phone, shouting*): Seven million, then!

POE: What? Me? Seven million?

B. D. (*on phone*): Nine million!

POE: Nine million?

DELIVERY BOY: Excuse me, I—

POE: Nine million? For me?

B. D. (*Looks at* POE. *Laughs. Turns to* TRISH, *who also laughs.*): Ha, ha, ha. That's a good one. (*on phone*) Okay, okay, twelve million tops.

POE: Not for me?

ASSISTANT: I've gotta get this contract out. What does this say?

TRISH (*reading*): "Two million dollars."

POE: Not for me?

TRISH: Silly boy. Have you forgotten? Five hundred—

POE: Dollars?

TRISH: Yes. Precisely.

DELIVERY BOY (*shouting*): Ex-cuse me! I think I made a mistake on the bill for the water. (*Fumbles in pockets, pulls out scraps of paper, which fall on* TRISH's *desk.* TRISH *eyes paper. Red lights still flashing.* B. D. *slams phone down, eyes the lights.*)

TRISH (*to* DELIVERY BOY): What are these?

DELIVERY BOY: Those? Just some poems I scribbled.

TRISH: Brilliant! B. D.?

POE (*weakly*): *Poems?*

B.D.: A discovery?

TRISH: Pre-cise-ly.

POE (*louder*): POEMS?

B. D.: A discovery!

ASSISTANT: A discovery!

TRISH: A discovery!

POE (*shouting*): POEMS???

TRISH: Delivery boy named—(*to* BOY) What is your name?

DELIVERY BOY: Me? Justin.

TRISH (*to* BOY): Where are you from?

DELIVERY BOY: Me? Jersey City.

TRISH: Brilliant!

TRISH and B. D. and ASSISTANT: Justin from Jersey City!

(*Single green light flashes, and continues to flash through end of scene.*)

POE (turns to audience, lowers voice): *Poems?*

Blackout.

Production Note for *The Raven*

As the stage directions indicate, the set is simple: a desk, two chairs, a bookcase, heaps of papers and manuscripts, and a wall or board plastered with Post-it notes. Both Trish's and Poe's chairs face the audience.

The flashing red and green lights add visual interest and humor and punctuate the increasing frenzy in the office. For a classroom performance, the lights can be as simple as four flashlights: two covered with transparent red film or tissue paper and two with green film/paper. Two students can operate these from behind a draped sheet (with holes cut for the lights) or even in full view of the audience. If they are in view of the audience, they should remain still, robotlike, so the attention is on the lights and not the people operating them.

—S. C.

THE BILLIONAIRE AND THE BIRD

(WITH MORE THAN A LITTLE THANKS
TO HANS CHRISTIAN ANDERSEN)

by KATHERINE PATERSON

CHARACTERS

REGINALD . . . . Valet and man-of-all work for Mr. Pombar

MR. POMBAR . . . . Third richest man in the world and number-one hypochondriac

SYLVA . . . . Young girl who helps out in the kitchen, age fourteen or so

HERMIT THRUSH . . . . . Small, grayish brown bird with a white speckled breast and rusty tail

Lights come up on the stage, revealing the opulent bedroom of
MR. POMBAR, *who is lounging in his California king-size
bed. He presses a buzzer at his bedside. The scurrying of feet
is heard outside the door and the valet,* REGINALD, *enters
carrying a tray and a bundle of papers and magazines.*

REGINALD: Your luncheon, sir.

MR. POMBAR: And just in time, too, Reginald. I was on
the verge of calling the highway patrol. What on earth
has been keeping you?

REGINALD: I was waiting for the mail, sir. It was late.

MR. POMBAR: Again? Remind me to buy the postal sys-
tem, Reginald.

REGINALD: Can you do that?

MR. POMBAR: As the third richest man in the world, I
can do anything I like.

REGINALD: If you say so, sir.

MR. POMBAR: Is that magazine here?

REGINALD: What magazine, sir?

MR. POMBAR: You know perfectly well what I mean. The
"um . . . um . . . let's spy on the filthy rich and famous"
one—what's it called?

REGINALD: I'm presuming you mean the *Periodical of
the Platinum People*, sir.

MR. POMBAR: Yes, yes, whatever. Has it come?

REGINALD: Here it is, sir. I've folded it over to the relevant page.

MR. POMBAR: Just tell me what it says while I eat my lunch. I'm sure you've read it already. . . . What's this blob here, Reginald?

REGINALD (*looking at the lunch*): A dollop of mayonnaise, I presume, sir.

MR. POMBAR: Mayonnaise? Horrors! Cook knows I loathe the very thought of mayonnaise.

REGINALD: Well, there's a new girl in the kitchen, sir—perhaps . . .

MR. POMBAR: Remind me to fire her. Take this away and dispose of it safely. It's nothing but a petri dish for potential putrefaction.

REGINALD: If you say so, sir. (*Takes the tray and starts toward the door.*)

MR. POMBAR: Not now, Reginald. You haven't read the article yet.

REGINALD (*confused*): But . . .

MR. POMBAR: Just put it on the windowsill. (REGINALD *obeys.*) Well, come on, come on, come on. What does it say? Was the fellow properly impressed with Neverending Acres?

REGINALD: He was indeed, sir. "The most astounding and extensive private forest in the world," I believe he said.

MR. POMBAR: Good. And the house itself.

REGINALD: Most impressed, sir. I believe "incomparable" was the exact word used.

MR. POMBAR: I'm sure they gave the gymnasium and entertainment wing high praise.

REGINALD: Indeed, sir.

MR. POMBAR: Did they mention the music hall?

REGINALD: Of course, sir. No one else in the country has an in-house symphony orchestra.

MR. POMBAR: I should think not. And what did the fellow like best of all my properties and possessions? The music hall, the spa, the entertainment wing? What? (REGINALD *is hesitating*.) That fool writer always names a most coveted possession, doesn't he? What did he choose?

REGINALD: I don't understand it, sir. It's something I hadn't heard about before.

MR. POMBAR: Not heard about? Well, what on earth is it?

REGINALD: A hermit thrush, sir.

MR. POMBAR: A what?

REGINALD: It's a little bird, sir. Apparently it has a beautiful song. At any rate, the journalist was quite taken with it.

MR. POMBAR: What nonsense! Out of all my vast and valuable possessions he chooses some jaybird.

REGINALD: Thrush, sir.

MR. POMBAR: Thrush, mush. Who cares? I never heard of it.

REGINALD: Well, you will now. The telephone has already begun ringing—bird lovers from all over the country asking permission to come hear the song of your remarkable bird. Even Will Yates called.

MR. POMBAR: Yates called? What does that popinjay want? I suppose he's after my bird.

REGINALD: He didn't say that, sir. He said he just wanted to hear it sing.

MR. POMBAR: Humph. That writer fellow didn't happen to tell you where in Neverending Acres he saw the bird, did he?

REGINALD: He never actually saw it, sir. Just heard it.

MR. POMBAR: Well, someone must have seen it. We've got to catch it. And, Reginald, we need a cage. There must be one around here somewhere. And hurry. I don't want to miss a chance of one-upping that scoundrel Yates. You know the help, Reginald. Get some of the men to bring it in.

REGINALD: I've already asked around, sir, and nobody seems to have actually seen the bird except . . . except the new girl in the kitchen.

MR. POMBAR: The mayonnaise glopper?

REGINALD: Yes, sir. That would be the one. She lives with her father, who is one of the foresters. Apparently she and this bird are—uh—quite friendly. When I mentioned this strange paragraph in the article, she seemed to know all about the bird.

MR. POMBAR: Well, then tell the girl to bring it in. She'll be no loss in the kitchen, that's evident.

REGINALD: Anticipating your request, sir, I took the liberty of sending her out some time ago. She should be back anytime now.

MR. POMBAR: I hope you also had the sense to send some of the men to help her locate it.

REGINALD: I tried to, sir. But she said there was no need. That the bird usually appears when it sees her in the forest.

MR. POMBAR: Is she some kind of witch?

REGINALD: No, sir. Just a very ordinary sort. Uh—would you be dressing before the girl arrives, sir?

MR. POMBAR: Of course not. I'm not at all well. I'm too ill to dress. You know that perfectly—

(While they have been talking, the lovely song of a bird has been heard outside the window. Both men hear it and stop to listen.)

MR. POMBAR: What are you waiting for, man? Open the window!

(REGINALD hurries to obey, opening first the window, then the door, ushering in SYLVA. A small grayish brown bird, the THRUSH, perches on the windowsill, still singing its heart out.)

REGINALD: The girl . . .

MR. POMBAR: Hush, man. Listen!

(SYLVA goes over to the window. The two men are rapt. We see MR. POMBAR wipe his eyes with the edge of the top sheet. The singing stops.)

MR. POMBAR (*quietly*): Go on—don't stop.

SYLVA: He wants to thank you.

MR. POMBAR: Thank me? Whatever for?

SYLVA: It made him very happy to think that his song made you cry.

MR. POMBAR: Yes. Very peculiar. I haven't wept since . . . I don't remember when. I must have been a boy. I can't think what came over me.

SYLVA: It's okay. I often cry when he sings. He doesn't mind. In fact, it makes him happy to see tears. They let him know that he has brought something really beautiful into the world.

MR. POMBAR: How do you know what it thinks? It's a bird, after all. And you're nothing but a child—a girl at that.

SYLVA: I don't know how. I just know. . . . Oh . . . He says to tell you "good-bye." He'll be going now.

MR. POMBAR: No, no. It mustn't go. Tell it to stay.

SYLVA: He needs to rest after all that singing. He promises to come back before too long.

(The THRUSH *flies away.)*

MR. POMBAR *(to* REGINALD*)*: I told you to get a cage.

SYLVA: You can't cage him, Mr. Pombar! Nobody can. Don't even think of it, or you'll never see him again.

MR. POMBAR: Most unsatisfactory, I'd call it. What use is it to own a bird that doesn't do what you tell it to?

SYLVA: You can't own any wild bird, Mr. Pombar, and certainly not this thrush.

MR. POMBAR: Who are you to order me around, girl? I will not be told what I can or cannot do with my own property. Now get back to your pan handling, and take that miserable mayonnaise-contaminated tray out with you when you go. I can already hear the bacteria bubbling up on that arugula. . . . (*He sighs.*) Oh, leave me in peace. (*He lies back against his mountain of pillows and closes his eyes.*) I am not a well man.

(SYLVA *picks up the tray and beats a quiet but hasty retreat.* REGINALD *plumps a few pillows and straightens the bedclothes, every now and then glancing at the open window, then goes over and gently closes it and pulls the curtains across to darken the room.*)

MR. POMBAR: What am I to do, Reginald? I already miss the stupid bird.
REGINALD: She said he'd come back again, sir.
MR. POMBAR: Yes, but, when? When? There's no schedule, no agenda. I might be asleep—or who knows, I might be downstairs or out of the house altogether. . . .
REGINALD: That's hardly likely, sir, since you haven't left this bed for more than a few minutes since last January.
MR. POMBAR: I'm not a well man, Reginald. You know that.
REGINALD: No, sir. I mean, yes, sir, I'm quite aware—
MR. POMBAR: The strange thing is . . . You won't believe this, Reginald—I hardly believe it myself, but when that ugly little bird was singing, I felt almost . . . like a . . . like a boy again.
REGINALD: I do believe it, sir. I, too, had a strange sensation of youth and well-being as—

MR. POMBAR: I could cage it, you know. I have every right.

REGINALD: Yes, sir. But the problem remains . . .

MR. POMBAR: What problem?

REGINALD: It seems that no one but the girl has ever actually seen the creature in the wild, much less come close enough to catch him.

MR. POMBAR: I've built an empire on solving unsolvable problems, Reginald. I won't let that minor detail stop me.

REGINALD: No, sir. Not to be impertinent, sir, but just how—

MR. POMBAR (*waving his hand*): I'll think of a way! I didn't become the CEO of fourteen international conglomerates by saying "can't"! Now, no more talk of problems, no more talk of defeat, you hear?

REGINALD: Absolutely not, sir.

MR. POMBAR: Uh, Reginald. The girl says the bird tells her things. Have you ever heard of a talking bird?

REGINALD: Only once, sir.

MR. POMBAR: And when was that?

REGINALD: It was, uh, in a poem, sir. By a Mr. Poe. A Mr. Edgar Allan Poe. I think you'll recall it from your own school days.

MR. POMBAR: "The Raven"?

REGINALD: "Quoth the raven, 'Nevermore.'"

MR. POMBAR: If this is your idea of a jest, Reginald, I do not, under the circumstances, find it the least bit amusing.

REGINALD: I do beg pardon, sir, I was only—

MR. POMBAR: The fact is that I named this estate Never-ending because I viewed it as an eternal Eden, so vast, so opulent, so magnificent, so . . . so enormously extensive that no one would ever find its end. Otherwise, the word "never" does not exist as part of my vocabulary. Alexander Portney Pombar never says "never." Certainly not in this particular case.

REGINALD: Indeed, sir. It was a very poor joke. I apologize.

MR. POMBAR: Now take your very unamusing self out of here and let me get some rest. I've had an exhausting morning.

(There is a very loud noise of a helicopter. REGINALD goes over to the window and pulls the curtain back to investigate.)

MR. POMBAR: Well, speak up, man, what is it?

REGINALD: It appears to be Mr. Yates's personal helicopter, sir.

MR. POMBAR: What in high heaven does that crook want? I've already told him I wasn't selling him a pencil, much less a corporation, a foreign market . . . or a bird.

REGINALD: I'll see, sir, right away. *(Pulls the drapes to.)* Will there be anything else, sir?

MR. POMBAR: Yes. Tell that cosmic thief I won't be seeing him. Just because he's the electronic emperor of world, he thinks I owe him an audience. I am not a well man, Reginald. I will never see him. Never! Do you hear me? Never!

REGINALD: Yes, sir. No, sir. I understand.

MR. POMBAR: It is past time for my nap. I am not to be disturbed.

REGINALD: No, sir. (*He tiptoes out of the room and closes the door behind him.*)

(MR. POMBAR *lies back in bed and begins to snore. Lights go down to show passage of time.*)

Outside the window of the darkened bedroom the song of the THRUSH *can be heard.* MR. POMBAR *begins to stir until he wakes and sits up, turns on a light over his bed, and begins to ring his bell furiously.*

MR. POMBAR (*shouting*): Reginald! Reginald!

REGINALD (*entering*): Yes, sir?

MR. POMBAR: Open the window, man. The bird is back!

(REGINALD *hastens to pull drapes and open the window.*)

REGINALD: Will that be—

MR. POMBAR: Hush, man.

(*They are both silent, listening to the lovely song until it ends and the* THRUSH *flies away.*)

MR. POMBAR: Wait! I said, "Wait!" (*sadly, wiping his eyes*) It doesn't obey, you know.

REGINALD: Indeed. He does seem to have a mind of his own, sir.

MR. POMBAR (*lying back again*): Most unsatisfactory. Well, what is that rug rat Yates trying to hoodwink me into selling today? China? Japan? South Korea?

REGINALD: None of the above, sir. It seems to be just what he said before. He just wanted to hear the bird sing.

MR. POMBAR: Well, I hope the bird had sense enough not to comply.

REGINALD: I—uh—can't say, sir. Mr. Yates left in a terrible hurry.

MR. POMBAR: Call the girl.

REGINALD: Sylva, sir?

MR. POMBAR: Whatever she calls herself. Just get her in here. I trust she's scrubbed herself with antiseptic soap. She's handled mayonnaise, you know.

REGINALD: Yes, sir. Shall I leave the window open?

MR. POMBAR: Of course. As soon as you shut it, that stubborn little beast will take a mind to come back, and then I'll miss half the performance. (*He sighs deeply and pulls up the covers.*)

(*The* THRUSH *comes back and perches on the window-sill, cocks its head as if studying the figure in the bed.*)

MR. POMBAR (*muttering to himself*): Most unsatisfactory.

(*Suddenly the* THRUSH *begins to sing.* MR. POMBAR *gets carefully out of bed and tiptoes to be near the window. We can see that the* THRUSH *sees him, but it continues its song uninterrupted. Meantime, the door opens to reveal* REGINALD *and* SYLVA. SYLVA *stands there silently listening to the song.* REGINALD *is staring at* MR. POMBAR *with something like disbelief. The song ends.)*

MR. POMBAR (*very quietly*): Very nice. (*He turns to go back to bed and sees* REGINALD *and* SYLVA.) Harumph. (*He's wiping his eyes again.*) Yes, well, I . . . (*Trying to cover his embarrassment, he goes back to his bed and climbs in.*) I felt better there . . . for a minute. But it will pass. Feelings of well-being always do, you know.

REGINALD: If you say so, sir.

(REGINALD *busies himself rearranging the bedclothes and plumping the odd pillow. Meanwhile,* SYLVA *goes to the window and whispers something to the bird that we can't hear. The* THRUSH *nods and flies away.)*

MR. POMBAR: What's your name again, girl?

SYLVA (*turning from the window*): You mean me?

MR. POMBAR: I don't see any other girls in here, do you, Reginald?

REGINALD: Not at the moment, sir.

MR. POMBAR: Yes, of course, I mean you. What's your name?

SYLVA: Sylva.

MR. POMBA: Sylvia?

SYLVA: No, Sylva. S-y-l-v-a. I'm afraid my mother wasn't a very strong speller.

MR. POMBAR: That's evident but irrelevant. Did she have this same sort of—sort of—strange power over wildlife?

SYLVA: I don't understand.

MR. POMBAR: I mean was she able to summon birds on a whim? As you apparently can.

SYLVA (*confused*): Surely you don't think I call the thrush. If anything, he calls me.

MR. POMBAR: And just what does he call you?

SYLVA (*puzzled*): Huh?

MR. POMBAR: Never mind. You've got to understand that I need to be able to count on this bird. I need a schedule. Surely that can't be too difficult.

SYLVA: A schedule? For the bird?

MR. POMBAR: Yes, of course, for the bird. Look, here, young woman. I am not a well man. My doctor prescribes medications for me. On the bottle it tells me how many I am to take and at what time of day.

SYLVA: Are you thinking of the thrush as some kind of happy pill?

MR. POMBAR: Well. Yes. I feel better when it comes and sings. When it doesn't come, I feel worse. Is that clear enough for you? Therefore, I need it to appear on a regular, daily basis. Four times a day at a minimum . . . no, five. Yes, let's say five: morning, with each meal, and at bedtime.

SYLVA: Bedtime? You have a special time for going to bed? It looks to me as if you're always—

MR. POMBAR: Harumph. There would be a little something in it for you, of course—a kind of stipend—in addition to your regular salary.

SYLVA: You're not trying to bribe me, are you?

MR. POMBAR: What?!

SYLVA: Even if you were, it wouldn't help. It just doesn't work like that.

REGINALD: Perhaps if you explained to the bird that Mr. Pombar's health depended on its cooperation . . .

SYLVA (*shaking her head*): I really don't think—

MR. POMBAR: What does it matter what you think, girl? I own the bird. You work for me. Get that bird here five times a day, or . . .

REGINALD (*soothingly*): What Mr. Pombar means . . .

MR. POMBAR: I mean exactly what I say. Get the bird here five times a day, or there will be serious consequences for you and your wretched family. I employ both you and your father. I own that house you live in. I could blacklist you both from further employment. . . . And you could try a little more politeness in your speech. Like saying "sir" when you speak to me. (*He sinks back against his cushions.*) Go on, go on. Just get out of here. I need my rest. This whole situation has my heart racing out of control. I may have an attack coming on. You'll be the death of me yet, girl. Oh, what am I to do? What am I to do?

(SYLVA *exits quietly.* REGINALD *sighs and goes over to the window. He stares out of it as if hoping the bird will return. Then he quietly closes the window, pulls the drapes, and tiptoes out. The lights dim to show passage of time.*)

Lights come up to show MR. POMBAR *at the window, gazing out. There is a knock on the door.* MR. POMBAR *gets back into bed before answering.*

MR. POMBAR (*weakly*): Who is it?

REGINALD: Only Reginald, sir.

MR. POMBAR: Oh, come on in, man. . . . It hasn't come for days, you know.

REGINALD (*enters carrying a small box*): Did you mean the bird, sir?

MR. POMBAR: No, I meant the Transit of Venus. Of course I meant the bird. I don't think it's ever coming again. (*He sighs deeply.*) Remind me to fire the—what's her name—the rude child. Her father, too, while we're at it. (*Sighs again.*) Well, what did you want?

REGINALD: A special messenger has arrived from—from Mr. Yates.

MR. POMBAR: Yates? What does that *knuckleball* want this time?

REGINALD: He's sent a parcel for you, sir—a rather unusual parcel.

MR. POMBAR: I trust you had the bomb squad check it out.

REGINALD: Of course, sir. It is not dangerous—just peculiar.

MR. POMBAR: Why peculiar?

REGINALD: Well, it contains a . . . a bird.

MR. POMBAR: A what?!

REGINALD: No. No. Not your bird. It's some sort of new invention of his . . . an electronic bird.

MR. POMBAR: Why should Yates be sending me an electronic bird?

REGINALD: Perhaps the accompanying message would explain.

MR. POMBAR: Don't be coy, Reginald. You know perfectly well what it says.

REGINALD: Well, I did take the liberty . . . for security purposes, of course.

MR. POMBAR: Of course.

REGINALD: It seems that when he was here several months ago, he was able to digitally capture the song of the thrush.

MR. POMBAR: That scoundrel! How dare he? That song belongs to me.

REGINALD: He has put the song into this electronic bird . . .

MR. POMBAR: The nerve of that thief!

REGINALD: . . . so you could listen to it whenever you chose.

MR. POMBAR: I'll have him hauled into court! I'll sue! . . . I'll . . . What did you say?

REGINALD: It's electronic, sir. It can stay right beside your bed. All you have to do is clap your hands and it will begin to sing.

MR. POMBAR: You've tried it out?

REGINALD: I took the liberty . . .

MR. POMBAR: And it works?

REGINALD: Perfectly.

MR. POMBAR: Let me see it.

(REGINALD *takes the bird out of the box and carefully places it on the table beside the bed.* MR. POMBAR *picks it up. It is encrusted with sparkling jewels. He studies it carefully, then puts it down on the table.*)

MR. POMBAR: Well, it's handsome enough. But can it sing?

REGINALD: Try it, sir. Just clap your hands.

MR. POMBAR: Humph. (*He claps his hands. The song of the electronic bird begins. The men listen, entranced. It is exactly the same as the song of the hermit thrush.*)

MR. POMBAR (*wiping his eyes*): Well . . . well . . . quite the same, isn't it, Reginald?

REGINALD: It would seem so, sir.

MR. POMBAR: And much more satisfactory. You have to hand it to that rascal. He does come up with some clever ideas.

REGINALD: Indeed, sir.

MR. POMBAR: But never for free. What does he want this time? Did he say?

REGINALD: Well, in the message . . .

MR. POMBAR: Yes, yes.

REGINALD: First of all, he wishes for your good health.

MR. POMBAR: Baloney. He'd prefer me dead. What does he really want?

REGINALD: He suggested Japan, sir. . . .

MR. POMBAR: Japan? In exchange for this gewgaw? He must be out of his mind. Japan is my best market.

REGINALD: And South Korea.

MR. POMBAR: South Korea? Is he crazy?

REGINALD: Only if greed is insane. He also mentioned China.

MR. POMBAR: Now I know he's crazy. Next thing you know, he'll be demanding North Korea.

REGINALD: He did say that when that market opens up . . .

MR. POMBAR: Wait a minute! Wait just a micro minute. He sent me an unsolicited parcel. The law says I do not have to return unsolicited merchandise. I can keep it, and I'm under no obligation to pay for it. The bird is mine, Reginald. He has no more rights over it.

REGINALD: No, sir. The bird is yours. This one, that is.

MR. POMBAR: What do you mean, "this one"?

REGINALD: Well, the message goes on to say that if you do not turn over the Asian markets to him, he will mass-produce the bird and flood the world with them.

MR. POMBAR: He'll what? But that would mean any fool on earth could have a bird exactly like mine!

REGINALD: Yes, sir. Minus the jewels, of course.

MR. POMBAR: I'll copyright the song. I should have thought of that before I let that vulture Yates onto my property.

REGINALD: I'm not sure that one can copyright a wild bird's song, sir.

MR. POMBAR: Of course I can. Anything is copy-rightable.

REGINALD: If it is—and I rather doubt that, sir—don't you imagine Yates took out a copyright when he made the prototype for this one?

MR. POMBAR (*sighing*): No doubt he did. He thinks of everything, that swine. Oh, Reginald, what am I to do? I'm not a well man, you know.

REGINALD: No, sir. I know, sir.

(MR. POMBAR *lies back against his pillows and claps his hands. The electronic bird begins to sing. Both men listen intently, not noticing that the* THRUSH *has landed on the windowsill. It listens, shakes its head, and flies away.*)

MR. POMBAR: Oh, have the lawyers draw up the papers, Reginald. Give Yates whatever he demands. I'm not sharing this bird with another soul on earth.

REGINALD: Are you sure, sir? That's rather a lot of—

MR. POMBAR: Never question me, Reginald. Do you hear me? Never!

REGINALD: No, sir. I'll get everything in order right after I see to lunch.

MR. POMBAR: Lunch can wait. Call the lawyers at once.

REGINALD: Wouldn't you like to sleep on it, sir? Just give the matter a little more thought before . . .

MR. POMBAR: I'm warning you, Reginald.

REGINALD: I'm on my way, sir. (*He exits hurriedly.*)

(MR. POMBAR *claps his hands and listens happily to the electronic bird singing. When the song is done, he claps his hands and it sings again. He does this several times. There is a knock on the door. He ignores it at first. The knock is repeated a little louder.*)

MR. POMBAR: I told you to call the lawyers, Reginald. Now go away and do what you're told.

SYLVA (*opening the door a crack*): It's not Reginald. It's just me. With your lunch. (*She enters as song winds down. She glances at the window, which is empty.*) Oh. I thought the thrush was here.

MR. POMBAR: Didn't I fire you?

SYLVA: No. Not that I know of.

MR. POMBAR: Well, remind me to do that. But first, let me show you something. (*He claps his hands, and the electronic bird begins to sing. They both listen until the song ends.*)

MR. POMBAR: What do you think of that, little missy?

SYLVA: It's quite . . . quite clever, I guess.

MR. POMBAR: Yes. Even if Yates did invent it. You have to hand it to him. He's got the song exactly.

SYLVA: And it's . . . it's an eyeful, to be sure.

MR. POMBAR: That's the jewels. A small fortune in gems. Quite outshines your little brown friend, eh?

SYLVA: If you like that sort of thing. Of course . . .

MR. POMBAR: Of course what?

SYLVA: Well, it may just be me, but I like the real bird better.

MR. POMBAR: Nonsense. That bird is totally unsatisfactory—comes and goes as it pleases and is ugly as a mud puddle. How could you prefer it to this lovely thing?

SYLVA: Maybe because that one is as dead as a dustpan. No feelings at all. It doesn't matter to it if you are sad or happy. It doesn't care if it makes you cry or not.

MR. POMBAR: Why should it bother me if it has no feelings? It looks gorgeous and it sings whenever I clap my hands.

SYLVA: Yes. But . . .

MR. POMBAR: But what, you insolent girl?

SYLVA: Nothing.

MR. POMBAR: Speak up!

SYLVA: I was just wondering . . . well, I was wondering why it doesn't make you cry when you hear it sing.

MR. POMBAR: Well of course it makes me cry. Exactly as I did for your little squab.

SYLVA: Well, I couldn't help but notice that you weren't crying just now when you showed it to me.

MR. POMBAR (*realizing she is right*): Well, I did earlier. But who wants to spend one's life weeping? I've grown accustomed to its singing. I'm enjoying it. I don't have to bawl like a baby every time it opens its little golden beak, now, do I?

SYLVA: No, of course not. I was just wondering, that's all. Will there be anything else?

MR. POMBAR: You didn't put mayonnaise on my salad, did you?

SYLVA: How could I? You'd have to go at least fifty miles from here to find a jar of mayonnaise. I wonder why that is.

MR. POMBAR: Humph. By the way, I may not fire you after all. Not today, anyway.

SYLVA: That's mighty kind of you.

MR. POMBAR: And you can tell that silly bird of yours not to bother coming again. I don't need it anymore.

SYLVA: I don't think you need to worry about that. He knows when he's not wanted.

(*As* SYLVA *exits,* MR. POMBAR *claps his hands and listens to the electronic bird's song while he starts to eat his lunch. He is humming as the lights dim to show passage of time.*)

When lights come up, MR. POMBAR *is reading a newspaper. He stops long enough to clap his hands. The electronic bird begins to sing. He smiles and continues reading. There is a knock on the door.*

MR. POMBAR: Yes? Who is it?

REGINALD: It's I, sir. (*Opens the door.*) With a message.

MR. POMBAR: Well, come in, man. (REGINALD *is obviously hesitating.*) Out with it. What kind of message?

REGINALD (*entering*): It's from Mr. Yates, sir.

MR. POMBAR: He cannot have Southeast Asia. A bargain is a bargain. Tell him that.

REGINALD: He doesn't actually want anything, sir.

MR. POMBAR: Don't be naive, Reginald. The joker always wants something.

REGINALD: Well, he'd—he'd like to give back Japan.

MR. POMBAR: What's the matter with Japan?

REGINALD: Nothing, sir, as far as I know.

MR. POMBAR: Then what's his game this time? Japan's the best market.

REGINALD: It's not Japan, sir—it's—it's—well, it's the bird.

MR. POMBAR: I'm never giving it back and that's final.

REGINALD: He isn't asking for it. It's just that—well, you said so yourself, sir. A bargain is a bargain.

MR. POMBAR: What are you getting at, Reginald? Stop tiptoeing around the thicket and get on with it. . . . Now!

REGINALD: It wasn't Mr. Yates, sir. He swears to that. It was one of the technicians. The man has already been fired.

MR. POMBAR: Go on.

REGINALD: Well, it seems they destroyed all copies of the originally recorded song—as you demanded in the contract.

MR. POMBAR: I should certainly hope so.

REGINALD: And there's a problem . . .

MR. POMBAR: What kind of problem, Reginald? Out with it.

REGINALD: It's the chip, sir. The one that makes the bird sing.

MR. POMBAR: Nonsense. It works perfectly. See? (*He claps and the electronic bird begins to sing.*)

REGINALD: You might not want to do that, sir. At least, not so often.

MR. POMBAR: What are you talking about, Reginald? I can do it whenever I wish. (*He claps again.*)

REGINALD: It's the chip, sir. You see, the technician programmed it for . . . well, for a limited number of performances.

MR. POMBAR: What?!

REGINALD: It was not Mr. Yates's intention. He swears to it. The technician overstepped—

MR. POMBAR: What are you saying, Reginald? Exactly how many performances?

REGINALD: Well, no one is quite sure. Mr. Yates says if you activate it sparingly, it ought to last out several more months.

MR. POMBAR: Several more months!

REGINALD: That was the message, sir.

MR. POMBAR: But I haven't been activating it sparingly, Reginald. You know that.

REGINALD: Indeed, sir, you've been enjoying it with some frequency.

MR. POMBAR: This is outrageous! How am I to know when or how often I—

(There is a loud sound of clapping outside the door; the electronic bird begins to sing furiously.)

MR. POMBAR: STOP THEM, REGINALD!

(REGINALD rushes out of the room. The clapping ceases abruptly. The electronic bird slows down its song and eventually stops. MR. POMBAR is wiping his brow.)

REGINALD *(entering)*: I'm sorry, sir. It seems that the Cubs have just won the World Series. It was a spontaneous outburst from the staff, sir. I've warned them about clapping, sir. It won't happen again.

MR. POMBAR: It better not! I'll have their hides. . . . Oh, Reginald, what shall I do? I'm not a well man. I need this bird. My very life depends on it.

REGINALD: It is troublesome, sir. But perhaps, if you're very careful, very sparing in your usage . . .

MR. POMBAR: But how am I to know? I hardly dare . . . Oh, pull the drapes, Reginald. I need to rest. I don't feel at all well.

REGINALD: Yes, sir. *(Pulls the drapes closed.)* I'm very sorry about all this, sir. Will there be anything else?

MR. POMBAR: Yes. I want the entire Asian market returned, do you hear?

REGINALD: I'll see what I can do, sir.

(MR. POMBAR lies back in bed. He tosses and turns, sits up, starts to clap, stops himself just in time, sighing

deeply, pulls the covers over his head as the lights go out to show passage of time.)

Gradually a low light reveals in the bed the hunched body of MR. POMBAR. *The drapes are closed. The door opens silently and* REGINALD *enters, followed by* SYLVA. REGINALD *puts his finger to his lips and motions for* SYLVA *to come to the window.*

SYLVA: What's the matter with him?

REGINALD: I'm not quite sure. He's maintained for quite some time that he's not a well man . . .

SYLVA: Pooh. Just lazy, if you ask me.

REGINALD: Shh! I don't think he's bluffing this time. He hardly touches his food. He never says a word. He just lies there . . . curled up like that. I'm afraid—

SYLVA: Why doesn't he just clap his hands and—

REGINALD: He hasn't done that for days. I think he's terrified that he'll use up his last chances to hear the bird sing . . . and then . . . and then . . .

SYLVA: And then what?

REGINALD: And then he'll just . . . die.

SYLVA: Really?

REGINALD: I'm guessing. I don't really know. . . . Oh, I know he's a tyrant, and a bit of a blowhard, but I am rather fond of him.

SYLVA: You're a good person, Reginald. Not many people would care about a guy like that.

REGINALD: Well, he's always been good to me, you see.

SYLVA: I see you've always been good to him. He doesn't deserve a friend like you.

REGINALD: Well, if you won't do it for him, would you do it for me? Call the bird, I mean. The real one.

SYLVA (*sadly*): You forget, Reginald. I can't just clap my hands and call the thrush. It doesn't work that way.

REGINALD: I know. But whatever influence you might have . . .

SYLVA: Sometimes . . . sometimes he comes because he knows he's needed. When my mother died, he came all the time. Why don't you at least open the drapes. He'll know he's welcome then.

REGINALD (*hurrying to pull the drapes*): Oh, I do pray he understands the desperateness of the situation.

(*Light fills the room.* SYLVA *opens the window and leans out.*)

SYLVA: I can see him. He's coming.

REGINALD: Oh, thank God.

(*The* THRUSH *lights on the windowsill and begins its song.* MR. POMBAR *stirs, sighs happily, and sits up suddenly in alarm.*)

MR. POMBAR: Who clapped? Stop them!

SYLVA: It's all right, Mr. Pombar. No one clapped. He's back.

MR. POMBAR: You don't mean . . . the real bird? The thrush?

REGINALD: The very one, sir. He knew you needed him. So he came back—on his own—just like that.

MR. POMBAR: Hush, man. Have some respect. (*He is wiping his eyes. The song finishes, and the* THRUSH *flies away. Turning to* SYLVA) Will he come back again?

SYLVA: He comes and goes as he chooses. Not when anyone calls.

MR. POMBAR: Or claps.

SYLVA: Especially not then. But he may still be nearby. Why don't you come to the window? If he sees you—

MR. POMBAR: You mean get up? Surely, you're not suggesting that I get out of bed? For your information, missy, I am not a well—

SYLVA: I know. I know. You're not a well man. But he did come all this way. Just for you. It would be nice for him to know you appreciated it.

MR. POMBAR: You must be jesting.

SYLVA: You don't have to make a big deal of it. A simple "thank you" would do. Now, come on. It wouldn't kill you to say it.

MR. POMBAR (*sits up in bed*): Can you really see him out there?

SYLVA: Maybe—I can't be sure. What do you think, Reginald? Is that the thrush over there in that tree?

REGINALD (*going to window and peering out*): I'm not sure. Mr. Pombar, your eyesight is so much better than mine.

MR. POMBAR: It's been such a long time. (*He tentatively puts his feet over the side and then stands up. He is swaying.* SYLVA *and* REGINALD *rush toward him and keep him from falling.*)

SYLVA: Atta boy, Mr. Pombar. We won't let you fall. Now come along—he won't wait there forever. (*They walk him over to the window.*)

MR. POMBAR (*peering out the window*): There he is. I'm sure of it. That lovely little brownish body tucked in among the foliage. So what do I say?

SYLVA: "Thank you" would be nice. You do know how to say "thank you," don't you?

MR. POMBAR: Don't be impudent. Of course I do. Uh—uh—I'm grateful for—for—I do appreciate your . . . You have a lovely song. Quite lovely.

SYLVA: Well, it's a start. But you do need practice.

REGINALD: Oh, Mr. Pombar, you don't know how it does my heart good to see you standing on your own two feet again, sir.

MR. POMBAR: Don't make such a fuss, Reginald. And where the devil is my lunch, man? Suddenly I have the appetite of a ravenous beast.

REGINALD: Since you're already up, sir, may I be bold enough to suggest that it would make a nice change if you came downstairs for lunch?

MR. POMBAR: Downstairs? But, Reginald, you know I haven't been downstairs since— I'm not a well—

SYLVA: Better yet, Reginald, go ask Cook to fix us a picnic. We can take it into the forest. The thrush always comes when I go into the forest for a visit.

MR. POMBAR: Really?

REGINALD (*hesitating*): What do you say, sir? Would you be up to . . . ?

SYLVA: Of course he would. Nothing like good fresh air, is there, Mr. Pombar?

MR. POMBAR: I'm sure I don't know.

SYLVA: Then it's high time you found out. (*to* REGINALD) Come on, man, shake a leg.

(REGINALD *starts for the door.*)

MR. POMBAR (*Goes to the bedside table and picks up the electronic bird.*): Here, Reginald. Take this with you.

REGINALD (*Comes over and takes the electronic bird from* MR. POMBAR.): What do you suggest I do with it, sir?

MR. POMBAR: Oh, I don't know. The gems must be worth something. Get one of the lawyers to sell it. Anyhow, get it out of my sight.

REGINALD: Very good, sir. Shall I lay out your clothes before I go?

MR. POMBAR: No, I should be able to find them myself— that is, unless you've gone and given my entire wardrobe to the Salvation Army.

REGINALD (*smiling*): Might I be so bold as to suggest, sir, that that was a very poor joke?

MR. POMBAR: You do take liberties, Reginald. Now get on with it and let me dress for Sylva's al fresco repast.

SYLVA: It's only a picnic, Mr. Pombar . . . nothing special. Thanks to you, there won't even be mayonnaise on the sandwiches.

MR. POMBAR: Out! Out! Both of you. I need to get going. I have so much to catch up on—so much to do.

(As MR. POMBAR *goes to the closet and takes out clothes, the* THRUSH *appears at the window, studies the scene and begins to sing.* MR. POMBAR *turns and whispers "thank you" to the bird, wipes his eyes, and starts to remove his bathrobe as the light dims and goes out.)*

Production Note for
The Billionaire and the Bird

The only production difficulty I can foresee is the matter of the two birds. The actual hermit thrush might well be played by a puppet or person in the window, or a spot of light. Director's choice. The artificial bird doesn't have to do much but sit on the table. The same recorded hermit thrush song can be used for both birds. When everyone claps because the Cubs have won the World Series, which is perhaps the most fantastical element in the play, the birdsong could be speeded up to make it sound frantic after all that clapping.

—K. P.

THE
DOLLOP

by SUSAN COOPER

CHARACTERS

HARD HAT .... A construction foreman
ANNA .... A girl, age maybe twelve
TIME .... A boy, maybe ten
DECCA .... A girl, Time's twin
LUKE .... A boy, maybe eleven
JEN .... Anna's younger sister, maybe eight
DOLLOP .... A creature
GEORGE GREENFERN .... Time and Decca's father
SALLY GREENFERN .... Time and Decca's mother
MR. MOTT .... Anna and Jen's father
MRS. MOTT .... Anna and Jen's mother

Lights up. Nobody is onstage. Upstage right there might be a small tree or scrubby bush. Upstage left is a large mound of rock. Smooth, not jagged. A few tufts of long grass have somehow managed to grow out of it here and there.

(Suddenly a loud voice from offstage shouts through a bullhorn. It's HARD HAT, though we can't see him yet.)

HARD HAT *(off)*: You kids, get OUTA there! Can't you read? This is a hard-hat area. Get down outa that tree and get off this land, RIGHT NOW!

(Pause.)

I said NOW! Move, or I'm calling the cops!

(Pause.)

AND DON'T COME BACK!

(Five children come running onto the stage and collapse near the rock, panting. ANNA is the eldest, perhaps the biggest: confident bordering on bossy. TIME—boy—and DECCA—girl—are fraternal twins: TIME the more practical of the two, DECCA more emotional. Then

there's low-key LUKE *and* ANNA's *younger sister,* JEN, *the smallest of the four.)*

ANNA (*tragic*): That's the *last time* we shall ever climb our tree! The very last time!

TIME: We could come back when they've gone.

DECCA: They're not going, Time, not ever! They're cutting our tree down!

LUKE: They're cutting them all down. That's what always happens.

ANNA: They're just bulldozing everything! The whole woods will be gone!

TIME (*looking out and down, offstage right*): They've cut down the trees around the pond already. It looks bigger.

LUKE (*joining him*): Everything goes. It's awful. He'll skin the land before he builds the houses.

DECCA: Who?

LUKE: The developer. That's what they do. I saw it back where I used to live. Did you see those little orange flags near the pond? That's where the first houses will go. They're already digging holes for the foundations.

(HARD HAT *comes bustling across the stage from stage left, hard hat on head, bullhorn in hand. He pauses when he sees them. They scramble to their feet.*)

HARD HAT: You still here?

ANNA: We're not in anyone's way.

HARD HAT: You're trespassing.

TIME: This bit isn't yours—it belongs to the town.

HARD HAT: The developer's buying it from the town. Go home.

DECCA: We're not doing anything wrong.

HARD HAT: Go play on the beach. It's more fun. My kids play on the beach all the time.

(They stare at him in hostile silence. We hear one of those irritating noises cell phones make, and HARD HAT pulls a cell phone off his belt and answers it.)

HARD HAT: Hello? . . . Oh, it's you, good. Listen, we keep hitting rock, we're gonna have to blast. . . . Tomorrow morning. Make sure we got a permit. And call the cops—they'll have to close the street. Have some signs made. . . . Okay—get back to me. *(He snaps the cell phone shut and looks at the children. He's not a bad guy, just very busy.)* Look, kids, it's gonna get dangerous around here, understand? Nobody wants you to get hurt. *(He catches sight of LUKE.)* Luke! Is that you? You should know better. Get your friends out of here.

LUKE: We were just watching.

HARD HAT: When I come back, you guys had better be gone. Go play on the beach.

(He hurries offstage, thumbing a new number on his cell phone.)

DECCA *(mocking)*: "Go play on the beach."

ANNA *(to LUKE)*: He knows you, Luke?

LUKE: My dad knows him. I think he's the foreman down there.

ANNA: I can't *believe* they're doing this. That's our place—we've been coming here since we were born, practically. Why do they have to build houses there?

(TIME *is looking offstage, craning his neck.* JEN *clambers a little way up the mound of rock and begins picking a tiny bouquet of grass stems, one by one.* ANNA *glances at her, big-sister protective.*)

ANNA: Don't go near the edge, Jen.

JEN: I'm not.

TIME: (*looking off*): They've got as far as our tree! Don't look, Decca—you don't want to see this.

(*The others join him—all except* JEN.)

DECCA: Are they going to chop it down? Now?

LUKE: Looks like they're going to knock it down.

DECCA: *Knock* it down? That huge great tree?

TIME: Look at the size of that backhoe! Oh, wow—

LUKE: They'll never make it—

ANNA: Our poor poor tree—look, it's leaning over—oh, its roots are coming out of the ground—it's going down!

DECCA: Oh no!

(*They're all caught up in watching, tense; from their body language you can almost see the tree falling, falling, falling, until—*)

TIME: There it goes!
ALL: Aaaaaaaw!

(They stand there sad and limp, looking out at the unseen fallen tree. Upstage, as JEN reaches for another stem of grass, the whole area of rock beneath her shifts a little. JEN freezes. The rock moves again.)

JEN *(frightened)*: Anna!

(The others turn to look at her.)

ANNA: What is it?
JEN: This rock's moving!

(The rock rises slowly, to a point at which JEN— who has been frozen in terror—slides down off it. She scuttles over to ANNA, who puts her arms around her. We begin to hear a sound like slow heavy breathing. The children stand together staring, instinctively moving a little closer to one another. The area of rock moves gradually higher and then is still. The children gasp.

The rock speaks in a hoarse, blurry voice. It is the DOLLOP, and it is made up of at least ten actors, maybe twenty. They are completely covered by sackcloth, cardboard, a sheet, whatever can make them look like one large object. Until ANNA said "What is it?" they were all hunched down; it was the movement of their slowly getting to their feet that made JEN slide off their covering.

The voice of this chorus is very slow and creaky, and—if possible—fairly deep.)

DOLLOP: Dol—lop.

(DECCA shrieks and clutches TIME.)

DECCA: It's talking! It's a rock, and it's talking!
ANNA: That's impossible!
DOLLOP: Dol—lop.
TIME: This isn't happening. This can't possibly be happening.

(This time the DOLLOP makes a softer, pleading noise, and there is a question in its voice.)

DOLLOP: Dol—lop?

(JEN detaches herself from ANNA and moves toward the DOLLOP.)

ANNA: Jen! Come back here!
LUKE: Be careful, Jen—
JEN: It's all right—I think it's just trying to tell us its name.
DECCA: A rock can't have a name!
JEN: This one has. Are you Dollop?
DOLLOP *(happily)*: Dol-lop . . . Dol-lop . . . Dol-lop . . .
TIME *(dazed)*: Rocks can't talk. Rocks can't move. Not on their own.
LUKE: Well, be realistic, Time. This rock is moving and talking. I think it likes Jen.

JEN: What's the matter, Dollop?

(*The* DOLLOP *shrinks down, as all the actors inside it get down again on their knees or crouch. It's now the same solid-looking mound it appeared to be at the beginning. For a moment it makes its sad pleading noise; then it becomes silent.*)

JEN: I think it's gone to sleep.

TIME: Gone to *sleep*?

LUKE: Makes sense. It's been sleeping for thousands of years and something woke it up. Think what a shock that must be. It's probably taking a nap.

TIME: Luke—come on, man—

DECCA: It's a rock. (*She crosses to it, cautiously, and stands looking down at it. Puts out a finger, thinks better of it, doesn't touch.*)

JEN: It's a sort of person. I like it.

ANNA: I think we're having a delusion. It's the shock of seeing our tree come down.

LUKE: The rock moved up out of the ground.

JEN: The Dollop.

LUKE: The Dollop. It came up. And then it went down again.

TIME: That's true.

LUKE: It moved. On its own.

DECCA: Well, maybe we're still in our delusion.

JEN (*admiring*): It's so big!

LUKE: It might stretch way down deep. D'you know what's the biggest living thing in the world?

ANNA: Oh, Luke—

LUKE: Come on. Guess.

DECCA: An elephant.

LUKE: No.

JEN: A woolly mammoth.

LUKE: They're extinct.

TIME: A whale.

LUKE: No.

ANNA: A banyan tree.

DECCA: A what tree?

ANNA: Banyan. In India. I saw a picture. It has about fifty trunks.

LUKE: Very good. Wrong, though.

DECCA: All right, cleversticks, what is it? What's the biggest living thing in the world?

LUKE: A mushroom.

(*The* DOLLOP *stirs a little.*)

ANNA: A mushroom? Oh, please.

LUKE: You can Google it if you don't believe me. It's an underground mushroom, it's in Oregon, it's two thousand years old, and it covers two thousand acres.

DOLLOP: Old. Old. Very old.

DECCA (*startled, jumping back*): Aah!

LUKE: There you are!

TIME: You think maybe he—it—is a mushroom too?

LUKE: No.

DOLLOP: Dol—lop.

LUKE: What I mean is, I think the Dollop is like that. Old. Ancient.

ANNA: Alive.

LUKE: Yeah. Just imagine you're him. It. Whatever. You lie here for thousands of years in peace, before the Pilgrims, before the Native Americans, and then these backhoes and bulldozers come roaring around. And a guy talks about blowing you up.

DOLLOP: Dollop get away. Danger. Help.

JEN: He wants us to do something.

DOLLOP: Danger. Old—friends—danger . . .

(ANNA, *having decided she has to believe in the* DOLLOP, *now speaks to it loudly and slowly as if to a half-witted foreigner.*)

ANNA: WHAT . . . FRIENDS . . . DO . . . YOU . . . MEAN?

DOLLOP: Old—old—old friends.

ANNA: Yes, but who are they?

TIME: Mushrooms, maybe.

ANNA: Oh, *Time*, enough with the mushrooms.

(*The* DOLLOP *makes an ominous growling sound.*)

JEN: We'll help you, Dollop.

LUKE: You want to get away.

DOLLOP: Yes. Yes. Get away.

DECCA: Why can't it just get up and go, then?

DOLLOP (*urgently*): Help. Help.

DECCA: I don't see why it needs us. It can move.

JEN: Not very much.

LUKE: Think about it. A rock walking down the road? The TV cameras would be buzzing around like flies.

ANNA: But what can we do?

TIME: If this land here wasn't in danger, it wouldn't have to move. The developer hasn't got this bit yet. That man, that foreman, he said they were *buying* it from the town—that means it's not theirs yet.

LUKE: There's been stuff in the paper. People want to stop him.

DECCA: Wasn't Dad talking about that the other night?

ANNA: This is urgent—let's check it out. Come on.

JEN: Don't go anywhere, Dollop. We'll be right back. Take a really long nap.

Blackout.

When the light goes up again, the DOLLOP *and the tree are gone.*

Downstage right TIME *and* DECCA *come to their father and mother,* MR. *and* MRS. GREENFERN, *who are sitting in chairs, reading.*

TIME: Dad, you know that new development near the common, where they're cutting down all the trees?

MR. GREENFERN: Do I ever. What a load of absolute—

MRS. GREENFERN (*warning*): George!

MR. GREENFERN: Vandals. That's all I was going to say. Vandals.

MRS. GREENFERN: Well. Yes, they are indeed.

DECCA: They knocked down our favorite tree today. That huge old maple. They're cutting all the trees!

MR. GREENFERN: So they can build another dozen McMansions. Yes. And they're trying to get some town land too—there's a public hearing about that tomorrow night. We have to go, Sally.

DECCA: Yes, you have to!

TIME: We should all go!

MRS. GREENFERN: We'll see. You certainly have to go, George. Throw some science at them.

TIME: You've got to stop them, Dad. Find a reason why they can't touch that land. Throw them a knuckleball.

DECCA: There could be something very old there.

TIME: Very very old. Huge. Like, d'you know what the old-est, biggest living thing on this planet is?

MR. GREENFERN: A mushroom.

TIME (*deflated*): Oh. Well yeah, I guess you would know.

MR. GREENFERN: Armillaria ostoyae. Honey mushroom. Friend of mine discovered a huge colony in Oregon. Covers more than two thousand acres.

TIME: There you go, then. There might be one on that land, so they shouldn't be allowed to touch it.

MR. GREENFERN: That mushroom's not the best example, buddy. It's a fungus, and it kills more trees than any developer. Feeds on their roots—wipes out whole evergreen forests over the years.

TIME: Oh.

MR. GREENFERN: Birds might be better ammunition. It's bird habitat. I'm going to bring that up at the meeting.

There's a lot of birdlife on that land—redtail hawks, some uncommon woodpeckers—even ravens—

DECCA: Suppose there was a very special rock there. Even older than the mushroom, really special.

MR. GREENFERN (*laughing*): Look, you two—you don't need to convince me. I've been fighting that developer for months. But he's hoodwinked everybody. Look at the tax money you'll get from people in my new houses, he says. In this town, money talks louder than biologists.

TIME: Is there anything that could stop him?

MR. GREENFERN: Not much. Maybe if we could show he's changing the water table, or making land subside. Anything that would mean the town had to pay money, instead of getting it.

DECCA: D'you think Anna's mom and dad will be at that meeting?

MRS. GREENFERN (*sighs*): I hope not.

MR. GREENFERN: Her father will, I'm afraid. He's on the town council. Not my biggest fan.

The light goes down on the Greenferns and up on another space downstage left, where ANNA and JEN are sitting with their parents, MR. and MRS. MOTT. MR. MOTT has a folder of papers. The Mott parents are much more pompous than the Greenfern parents, but ANNA and JEN are stuck with them.

ANNA: It was a wonderful old tree. We used to take books up into it and read.

MR. MOTT: People need new houses, honey—you can't let a tree get in the way.

MRS. MOTT: You're too old to be climbing trees, Anna. You could break an ankle, and then what would happen to your tennis?

JEN: I'M not too old.

MRS. MOTT: You're too young.

JEN: Oh, Mom!

MRS. MOTT: Don't "oh, Mom" me. Parents do know best about some things.

MR. MOTT: I'll tell you girls a secret—we're thinking of moving to one of those big new houses when they're built. How about that! You'd each have your own bedroom!

ANNA: Trees are more important than bedrooms.

JEN: And so are rocks. Very big old rocks.

MRS. MOTT: You two spend too much time with those Greenfern twins.

MR. MOTT: George Greenfern's kids?

MRS. MOTT: Yes. They're as tree-huggy as their parents. Can you imagine christening a boy Time?

ANNA (*coldly*): His real name is Justin. It's a joke. They call him Time because his dad said he arrived just in time.

MRS. MOTT: That's no way for an adult to talk to children.

ANNA: Oh, Mom!

MRS. MOTT: Stop that!

MR. MOTT: Now, now—calm down, everyone. I have to write my talk for Sunday's meeting. Where I shall waste a lot of time listening to George Greenfern bleat about birds and trees, I expect.

MRS. MOTT: Oh—the public hearing. I'd forgotten.

ANNA: What's it about?

MR. MOTT: Nothing very interesting.

ANNA: *What's it about*, Dad?

MR. MOTT: Well, if you must know, it's about the new development. There's a bit of fuss over the land, but it won't amount to anything.

ANNA: The developer wants the land next door as well, doesn't he?

JEN: He wants the land with the rock, and he can't have it!

MR. MOTT: What rock?

ANNA: Quiet, Jen.

MR. MOTT: I don't know what you're talking about. This town needs to grow. People like the Greenferns can't get in the way of progress—we'll vote them down. I see that developer at the country club. He's a good man—he's the mayor's brother-in-law!

Blackout.

When the lights come up, the children are back with the DOLLOP.

ANNA: Wake up, Dollop! Wake up!

JEN: We have to do something! Parents are useless!

DECCA: Wake up, Dollop!

DOLLOP: Dol—lop.

TIME: Yes, we know that.

DOLLOP: Dollop get away. Dollop get away.

LUKE: Yeah, sure, but we can't do it for you. You're going to have to move.

(*The* DOLLOP *shifts just a little. It gives out a long moan.*)

JEN: Come on, nice Dollop, clever Dollop, you can do better than that.

(*The* DOLLOP *makes a heavy-breathing noise and remains still.*)

LUKE: If we could just get him to the edge of the slope, he could roll all the way down the hill. There's nobody there now—they've stopped work for the day.

TIME: But what good would that do? They're going to blast rock down there, you heard what that man said—they'd blow him up!

ANNA: If he stays here, we absolutely *have* to stop the developer getting this piece of land.

JEN (*unhappily*): Daddy likes the developer.

DECCA: Our dad said we can only stop the developer if he changes the water table. Whatever that means.

LUKE: If he causes a flood. That's what it means, more or less.

(*They all stand stage right looking offstage, down the hill at the development. Thinking. The* DOLLOP *lets out another long sigh.* JEN *goes over and pats it consolingly.*)

ANNA (*suddenly*): Ahhh! (*She's had an idea; she points down the hill. They look at her, and wait.*)

TIME: Well?

ANNA: The pond. Down there in between the first three houses.

LUKE: He calls it a lake. He's very proud of it.

TIME: Who does?

LUKE: The developer.

TIME: It's a pond.

LUKE: Of course it is.

ANNA: But it's big—if the Dollop rolled into it, there'd be a flood!

DECCA: She's right!

TIME: They'd just pull him out.

ANNA: They wouldn't know he was there, if he was under the water!

JEN: Dollop, how do you feel about water?

DOLLOP: Dollops love water. Water is old. Dollops *love* water!

(Everyone crosses to the DOLLOP. They stand around him.)

ANNA: Okay, Dollop, we know how to save you. You have to get up out of the ground.

(The DOLLOP groans.)

TIME: One—two—three! *(He beckons the others; they join in.)*

ALL: One—two—three—UP!

(The DOLLOP doesn't move. They try again, conducted by TIME.)

ALL: One—two—three—UP!

DOLLOP: Dollop needs help. Dollop needs help.

ANNA (*exasperated*): What do you expect us to do—pick you up?

DOLLOP: Ask Jen. Ask Jen.

ANNA: Am I crazy, or did it say "Ask Jen"?

DECCA: Yes, it did.

(*They all look at little* JEN *with a mixture of astonishment and respect.*)

JEN: Well—if we, like, *think* him up. Think about him getting up. It would help him. Close our eyes and sort of see a picture of him getting up.

LUKE: Concentrate.

JEN: Yes.

TIME (*mocking*): The Power of Thought.

DECCA: Well, it's worth trying.

TIME: Okay. Why not?

ANNA: Here goes, then. Let's concentrate, for ten seconds. I'll count.

(*They all hold hands and close their eyes.*)

ANNA: One steam engine . . . two steam engines . . . he's getting up, think of him getting up . . . four steam engines . . . five steam engines . . .

(*Gradually, the* DOLLOP *begins to grow as it rises out of the ground.*)

ANNA (*cont.*): . . . six steam engines . . . seven steam engines . . . eight steam engines . . . nine steam engines . . . ten steam engines!

(*They all drop hands and open their eyes—and jump backward, startled.*)

DOLLOP: Eleven steam engines . . . twelve steam engines . . .

(*The* DOLLOP's *voice takes over the counting, getting gradually louder and louder. And it's still growing. The children stand there staring. The* DOLLOP *grows and grows, taller and taller, still counting loudly. It towers over them. By the time it's reached its full height, it's almost shouting. It stops, silent.*)

TIME: Wow!

JEN (*delighted*): Look at you, Dollop!

LUKE: That's amazing!

DECCA: He's so big—he'll almost fill that whole pond!

ANNA: Over here, Dollop—this way—

JEN: Come on, clever Dollop—you are the biggest rock I ever did see—come on—

(*They all encourage the* DOLLOP *as it sways across the stage to the far right.*)

ANNA: You just roll down the slope and into that pond. Lake. Whatever it is.

TIME: Then you can just stay there forever! You can go back to sleep! Safe under the water!

DOLLOP: Gooooood. Thank you. Thank you.

JEN: I'll miss you, Dollop.

DOLLOP: Thank you, Jen. (*Its tone changes.*) But . . . keep away, Jen. Keep away! Keep away!

(*Standing very still, it begins to make a low rumbling, growling sound. Suddenly it sounds ominous and angry. The growling gradually gets louder. This is not what the children expected. They back away slowly, toward the center of the stage. JEN is the last to move. She stays while the DOL-LOP's growl grows louder and louder—then she runs to ANNA, frightened. Now the DOLLOP speaks more clearly and confidently than it ever has before. Slow, loud, clear.*)

DOLLOP: *I am the Dollop, I am the avenger!*
I am coming!
I avenge the old things of the earth, I avenge the blasted rock and the dead tree!
I kill the destroyers!
Kill! Kill!

(*It lurches slowly offstage. It's shouting now. The children are frozen, watching.*)

DOLLOP: *Kill! Kill!*

(*The DOLLOP vanishes.*)

ANNA: No!
TIME: Who's he going to kill?
LUKE: Dollop, stop!

(From offstage there is a great crashing, clattering sound. The children run to look. They stare out offstage right.)

TIME: Look at him! He's smashed the tractor to bits!!
JEN: It's the machines he wants to kill, not people.

(Crash)

ANNA: He's squishing that truck like paper!

(Crash)

LUKE: There goes the big backhoe! Down into the lake!
DECCA: Now he's going after the bulldozer!
JEN: And the other backhoe!

(Enormous crash)

TIME: Yay, Dollop!
LUKE: Go get 'em, Dollop!

(Crash)

DECCA: There goes the last truck!
TIME: He's jumping in after them!

(*Drops of water splash over the children from offstage. They wipe their faces, shake the water off their clothes. Silence.*
They look down the slope, off.)

LUKE: Wow. They're all gone. Him too. Under the water.
DECCA: There's water everywhere.
TIME: Now it really is a lake.
ANNA: It's a flood. No house sites anymore. No little flags, no foundations.
TIME: No machines. No Dollop.
DECCA: Just water.
ANNA (*delighted*): He's beaten the developer!

(TIME *moves impulsively toward center stage and everyone follows except* LUKE.)

TIME: We have to get Dad! Take pictures for the meeting!
DECCA: They're going to be so psyched! The town won't sell him this land now—
TIME: And he sure won't be building houses over there—
ANNA (*happily*): My dad's going to be furious! He'll say (*She puts on a pompous voice.*) "Land development is Progress! What about the tax base!" He'll be so mad!

(JEN *laughs, claps her hands.*)

LUKE: So will mine.
DECCA: Is he on the council too?
LUKE: He's the developer.

(A silence. They all stare at him.)

TIME: Really?

LUKE (*awkwardly*): I didn't want to tell you. I mean—

JEN: That's all right. It's not your fault.

ANNA: We don't choose our parents.

DECCA: The Dollop smashed all his machines. Will he go bankrupt?

LUKE (*sadly*): Oh no. He's got insurance. He'll just go away and build more houses somewhere else. He'll say, "You win some, you lose some."

TIME: That's depressing.

LUKE: But maybe he'll be more careful about buying land with huge ancient rocks on it.

DECCA: And water.

JEN: And big old trees. The Dollop's friends.

(They all get quieter, thinking about that for a moment.)

ANNA: Remember our big old tree? That great long low branch, you could swing on it.

TIME: And the big branch farther up, where you could sit with your back against the trunk.

DECCA: You could climb really far—it was great for climbing.

LUKE: It was an awesome tree.

JEN: Well, there can be more trees.

ANNA: What?

JEN: There are little ones, right there. Look. By the hole where the Dollop used to be.

TIME: She's right. There's a whole row of them. Little maple trees.

LUKE: The wind must have blown the seeds up against the rock. Against the Dollop.

DECCA: He was looking after them.

JEN: Of course he was! So one day there'd be more trees for kids to play on.

TIME: It'll take years. Years and years.

LUKE: Well, it's better than nothing.

ANNA: We'll have to do it for him.

(ANNA turns to offstage right, and shouts.)

Dollop? We'll look after the trees, Dollop!

(Then she comes forward and looks at the audience.)

ANNA *(to audience)*: Won't we?

*(Maybe a few brave souls will say "Yes!"
ANNA frowns and shouts at the audience.)*

ANNA: WON'T WE?

AUDIENCE: Yes!

(The whole cast comes forward to face the audience.)

CAST: WE'LL LOOK AFTER THE TREES, DOLLOP!

(They make beckoning gestures, to bring out an answer.)

AUDIENCE: WE'LL LOOK AFTER THE TREES, DOLLOP!
CAST: WE'LL LOOK AFTER THE TREES!
AUDIENCE: WE'LL LOOK AFTER THE TREES!
CAST: WE'LL LOOK AFTER THE TREES!
AUDIENCE: WE'LL LOOK AFTER THE TREES!

(Once the audience is really shouting, the members of the cast stand there and applaud them. And, let's hope, the audience will applaud the cast.)

Blackout.

Production Note for *The Dollop*

The Dollop is the hardest part in this play. The five, ten, twenty actors of the chorus who play him can be made to look very much like a rock, or not at all. The most important thing is their voice, which must sound like one creature. They must rehearse saying their part together, A LOT. They also have to practice moving in unison. A useful qualification for a Dollop chorus member would be singing in a choir, playing in a band or orchestra, or playing a team sport.

One idea for a Dollop Rock look would be to stick together enough sheets of cardboard to make a "roof" covering all the actors (with holes for their fingers so they can hold it in place) and drape over it a king-size sheet. The Dollop has to grow as he emerges from the ground. He starts low, with the actors all crouched under their "roof," but when he grows big and tall at the end of the play, the actors must be standing with their arms and "roof" high over their heads—and their bodies and legs must still be covered by the sheet. If you're pretending to make him look like a rock, he shouldn't have visible feet.

If you like, the Dollop chorus can be just people, undisguised. In this case, since they will be visible all the time, they will have to work even harder to move in unison, like dancers. They will also have to work out some precise movements to cope with Jen when she climbs up on the "rock."

Any way of showing the Dollop is fine, so long as the audience will accept that it is a rock. That's the trick of all theater, in the end. You just have to make your audience "suspend disbelief."

When the Dollop has his revenge and begins destroying things offstage, the effect can be achieved by having people throw around any metal objects available, every stool or bench or pot or pan, handled with great noisy abandon.

Have fun!

—S. C.

EFFIGY
IN THE
OUTHOUSE

by RICHARD PECK

CHARACTERS

As many kids as you please, including these:

Three boys in a group—
WILLARD .... A big boy
CECIL .... A medium-size boy
JUSTIN .... A small, puny boy
EDNA WILBERFORCE .... A large, overbearing
eighth grader
MAE .... Edna's smaller sister; a screamer
FAYE .... Edna's smaller sister; a screamer
CECILIA SOPER .... A bedraggled girl
SMALL BOY .... Practiced in poultry

As many performers as you please playing adult parts.
They may be young people or actual grown-ups, including:

MISS DELILAH DOLLOP .... A fearful figure
MRS. WILBERFORCE .... Edna's mama
MISS NAOMI STARBODY ....A new teacher

Lights up on a one-room schoolhouse with a door and a window and two rows of benches facing the teacher's desk. Behind, a blackboard. On it are large chalk drawing of two privies, one labeled BOYS, *the other* GIRLS. *It is the first day of school in a long-ago faraway fall. A big boy stands stage center to address the audience.*

WILLARD: The school year I've been wanting to tell you about was 1901, here a while back. We went to a one-room schoolhouse. Ever hear of a one-room schoolhouse? Ours was the old Panhandle Ridge School, and it stood just south of the graveyard on Quagmire Road.

We were all jammed into the one room. And the big ones picked on the little ones, and the little ones told on the big ones. And all of us, big and little, were at war with the teacher.

Of course, it was just good, clean fun.

Summer died hard in our hearts. But in fact we couldn't wait for school to take up again every September. Especially in a year like this one, when we had us a new teacher coming. We'd already run off three teachers before I myself was in sixth grade. And this particular year, I was in sixth grade again.

We pupils were of the opinion that we did a service to the school board by weeding out the weaker teachers or anybody too young and inexperienced to keep us in line.

Anyway, a new teacher, name of Miss Naomi Starbody, was due, a young thing direct from the normal school where they trained new teachers.

Certain of us pupils were planning a reception for her that would send her packing before she found the chalk tray.

We made a point about being tardy, but never on the first day. Here three of us come now.

(*Lights up on the schoolroom as the speaker, WILLARD, falls back to join CECIL and JUSTIN. WILLARD is now carrying a melon with a ghastly face painted on it, wearing a farmer's cap. The puny one, JUSTIN, holds a polished apple. The medium-size one, CECIL, drags a human-size dummy stuffed with straw and dressed and booted as a hired man. It's wearing work gloves. CECIL drags it slow because he is slow.*)

WILLARD (*taking charge*): Men, we've got to move like the wind and get things set before Teacher turns up. What's our motto?

CECIL: You got me. Is it "Remember the *Maine*"?

JUSTIN: What's a motto?

WILLARD: Our motto is "Always take control before the teacher can." (*to* JUSTIN) What's in that apple, squirt?

JUSTIN: I hollowed it out at the core and packed it with three earthworms, two of them living.

(JUSTIN *crosses to plant the apple on Teacher's desk while the other two stuff escaping straw into the dummy.*)

WILLARD (*to* JUSTIN *at desk*): Squirt, whatever you do, don't open that drawer in Teacher's desk. Now scout around them shelves for something to attach this melon head to the effigy with.

CECIL: That's right. Paste or sumthun'. Lie-berry paste.

WILLARD (*to* CECIL): Cecil, you're dumber than any stump. Can a person paste a melon to straw?

JUSTIN (*rummaging*): How about twine?

WILLARD: Bring that ball of it. We'll tie the melon head on loose, so when Teacher opens the outhouse door, she'll see a man settin' in the female privy. *Then* his head'll drop off at sight of her. If Miss Starbody don't pass out of the picture entirely, she'll be in the next county and traveling with her skirt tails above her ears before that melon hits the outhouse floor.

CECIL (*sighing*): But what if she don't use the outhouse first thing? What if she holds out till noon?

WILLARD (*patiently*): Then we'll only have half a day of school.

CECIL: What if she holds off till the end of the—

WILLARD: Then we'll only have the one day of school.

(CECIL *ponders.* JUSTIN *looks back and forth between the bigger two as the scene dims.* WILLARD *steps forth to address the audience.*)

WILLARD: The effigy in the outhouse was one of our Panhandle Ridge traditions. But do I have to explain what an outhouse is? Those are drawings of them up there on the blackboard. That was our idea of art. We had two real ones behind the school, set over holes in the ground, right out by the graveyard fence. One outhouse was for the boys. The other was where the girls and Teacher sat.

(WILLARD *recedes to join* CECIL *and* JUSTIN. *They turn to some sound outside the window as the lights go up on the schoolroom.*)

EDNA (*hands on hips, booming*): Oh, for pity's sake, not the effigy in the outhouse again!
MAE and FAYE: Not again!
EDNA: If there's anything more predictable than three boys, I never saw it. You're as regular as death and taxes. And what do you think you're doing with those pages from the Sears catalog?

(WILLARD *is busy stuffing pages into the effigy's gloved hand.*)

WILLARD: If he's in the outhouse, he'd be holdin' paper, wouldn't he?
CECIL: Stands to reason. You don't want to be short of paper in there, and plenty of it.
JUSTIN: Them pages ain't sticking to the gloves, though.
CECIL: Better get you some lie-berry paste.

EDNA (*fetching up sighs*): Tell me you're not doing the rubber snake in the rafters again, are you? Not again this year!

MAE and FAYE: Not again this year!

WILLARD: Certainly not. What do you take us for?

EDNA: What's going on in that apple?

JUSTIN (*piping up*): Three earthworms, two living when they went in. When Teacher bites into them babies—

EDNA (*slapping her forehead*): You three are all dumb enough to squat with your spurs on. I declare, if you spent half the time on learning that you do on running off teachers, you'd all three be out of the second-grade primer by now. And get that melon-headed thing out of here. There's straw everywhere.

(*The pupils mill about, taking their time settling on the benches.*)

EDNA (*shaking free of* MAE *and* FAYE): And where's the teacher anyhow, that Miss Starbody? (*to* MAE *and* FAYE) You two go ring the bell.

MAE and FAYE (*whining*): Why?

EDNA: Because I say so.

MAE and FAYE: But why do we have to ring the bell? We're all here.

PUPIL'S VOICE: They's no teacher. Let's go on home.

ANOTHER VOICE: Let's go outside and play some catch.

ANOTHER VOICE: Let's break out our buckets and eat our dinners now.

ANOTHER VOICE: Let's go flush us some quail.

ANOTHER VOICE: Let's go over to the graveyard and smoke some cornsilk.

ANOTHER VOICE: Let's hold Justin's head under the pump.

EDNA (*taking up the teacher's pointer and fingering it grimly*): Nobody's going anywhere. I'll be Teacher till Miss Starbody gets here. I'm the oldest. I'm by far the smartest. My daddy has the biggest farm in the county. And I haven't repeated any grade, unlike some I could point out.

(*Her pointer points out* WILLARD.)

EDNA (*bristling importantly, to* MAE *and* FAYE): Get me the roll book and be quick about it. Stir your stumps.

(*As* MAE *and* FAYE *bustle up to Teacher's desk,* WILLARD *leaps up from the effigy.*)

WILLARD: Not the desk drawer!

(*But he's a moment too late.* MAE *and* FAYE *open the drawer, and a world of frogs leaps out.*)

MAE (*screaming*): Frogs! OOOH, they're spawning in there on the roll book or something.

FAYE: Nasty green ones.

MAE: It's like a swamp in there.

FAYE: We'll have warts!

MAE: One jumped in my pinafore pocket! Get it out!

(While they writhe and dance and shriek, WILLARD sags.)

WILLARD: It took me half the night to catch that many live. I had to use the net, not the sticker. *There's* a night gone out of my life I'll never get back.

(The schoolroom is already dissolving into chaos as all the pupils go to great balletic lengths to recapture the invisible frogs, falling over one another, bumbling into each other as they return them in cupped hands to the desk drawer. At last WILLARD, CECIL, and JUSTIN drag the effigy offstage, heading for the girls' privy. EDNA smacks the desk blows with Teacher's pointer time and again.)

EDNA: Onto your benches, every one of you, and I'm talkin' about right now. Stop all your rantin' and raven. I declare, you're all like hogs turned into an orchard. EVERYBODY SIT DOWN!
PUPIL'S VOICE: I'd sooner clear brush.
ANOTHER VOICE: I'd sooner eat hen grit.
EDNA (*howling*): SILENCE IN THIS SCHOOLROOM!

(The schoolroom scene dims behind the narrator as EDNA mimes teaching the slumping pupils in her heavy-handed way.)

WILLARD (*to audience*): Edna Wilberforce was no hand at teaching, but she dearly loved being up there in the teacher's place, laying about us with that pointer. Having no choice, the students let her. She had an arm on her like a blacksmith. Getting her to stop was more trouble than it was worth. She was like a hen who hates being pulled off the nest.

(*The room brightens behind* WILLARD *as he joins* CECIL *and* JUSTIN, *who creep back from planting the effigy in the outhouse, brushing straw off themselves. They settle on the bench farthest from* EDNA.)

CECIL (*ducking to* WILLARD): I still say we ought to have pulled the effigy's overalls down. After all, he's a-settin' on—

WILLARD (*knocking* CECIL *in the head*): He's all *straw*, you *knuckleball*. If we'd taken down his overalls, he'd have just blown away.

EDNA: Silence there on the back row!

JUSTIN (*to* WILLARD *around* CECIL): She surely does hope the real teacher won't turn up, don't she?

WILLARD (*in response*): It'd break her heart if she had one.

EDNA: COMPLETE SILENCE ON THE BACK ROW, OR I'LL SEND YOU FOR SWITCHES! Now it's time for arithmetic.

CECIL: Not arithmetic. I'd sooner eat—

WILLARD: How about current events? What happened to them?

EDNA (*moaning*): Oh, all right. Who has one?

A SMALL, BEDRAGGLED GIRL (*calling out*): What is one?

EDNA (*sententiously*): A current event is something that happened just here lately.

BEDRAGGLED GIRL: Oh, well shoot. I got one, then.

EDNA (*rubbing her forehead and making impatient sounds*): Come on up. You're new. Who are you, anyway?

(*The* BEDRAGGLED GIRL *comes forth and turns to class. She has a pronounced lisp.*)

CECILIA: I'm Cecilia Soper. Cecil's second cousin. Cecil Soper.

(*She points out* CECIL *and waves at him. He ducks down.*)

EDNA: Get on with it. What's your current event?

CECILIA: We all got ringworm from a litter of kittens this past Fourth of July. (*She ruffles through her hair with both hands, and everybody shies away.*) Aunt Madge had to rub Pond's Extract all over us day and night for a solid week.

(CECILIA *looks around to see that her story isn't going down very well.*)

CECILIA: Then we got ticks. So they had to soak us in a tick bath of creosote and soda and—

EDNA: Those aren't current events. They're disgusting. Sit down.

(CECILIA *wilts back onto her bench.*)

EDNA: A current event has nothing to do with infesta-
tions. A current event is like an election or a cyclone or
a battle.

WILLARD: Battle? Are we at war?

EDNA (*brandishing the pointer*): Come up here, and I'll
show you WAR. Besides, we're going to do arithmetic
now. Take out your slates.

(*Nobody does.*)

EDNA: If you can make a dollar a year off a hen, how long
would it take you to make twenty-two dollars with a hen
and a half?

PUPIL'S VOICE: A hen and a half? Where's the other half?

SMALL BOY (*rising and missing the point entirely*): Here's
how you raise hens. You feed them linseed meal so
they'll feather out good before the first frost. And if you
want good layers, you feed them on three parts bran,
two of corn chop, and one of bone meal. Throw in some
sunflower seeds.

EDNA: Sit down before I snatch you bald-headed. Let's try
spelling.

WILLARD: Let's not.

EDNA (*with menace*): Who can spell . . . (*She consults a
spelling book.*) . . . "substitute"?

WILLARD (*hand up*): I can't, but I can use it in a sentence.

EDNA: I doubt it, but try.

WILLARD (*standing up*): Edna Wilberforce thinks she's
the substitute teacher, but she ain't. I say if the real
teacher, Miss Starbody or whatever she calls herself,

doesn't turn up pretty durn quick, let's substitute this school day for a Saturday. (*Sits.*)

(*Pupils break into applause. EDNA brings her pointer down in the loudest THWACK yet.*)

EDNA: SILENCE IN THIS SCHOOLROOM! Who—if anybody—can spell the name of the president of these forty-five United States?
JUSTIN (*his hand wavering in the air as everybody looks at him*): I might be able to.
EDNA: I doubt it, but try.
JUSTIN (*standing*): Capital W-i-l-l-i-a-m capital M-c capital K-i-n-l-e-y. That's the way to spell it. Here's the way to yell it: WILLIAM McKINLEY!

(*After this sudden performance, he sits. A thoughtful silence lingers while everyone including EDNA wonders if JUSTIN got the spelling right. He looks around, waiting for approval. In the silence comes a riveting sound: the squeaking of a door far offstage. Everybody jumps.*)

WILLARD: That was an outhouse door!
CECIL: It's the girls' outhouse. I'd know that squeak anywhere.

(*MAE and FAYE scream. Then a tense silence from all as they strain to hear more.*)

WILLARD: She ought to have seen the effigy in there by now.

CECIL: Unless she sat down on his lap.

WILLARD: Nobody's that absentminded, not even a teacher.

(All the pupils nearest the window leap from their benches and gang together to look out in the direction of the girls' outhouse.)

PUPIL AT WINDOW: She ain't a-going in. She's a-coming out.

ANOTHER (FEMALE) PUPIL AT WINDOW: She's turned back, latching the outhouse door. It bangs if you don't.

ANOTHER PUPIL AT THE WINDOW: She's headed over to the willow tree. *(Pause.)* She's hiking her skirts. *(Pause.)* She's pulling something out of the elastic on her step-ins. *(Pause.)* It looks like a jackknife.

ANOTHER PUPIL AT THE WINDOW: Heaven help us! She's cutting switches!

(MAE and FAYE scream.)

ANOTHER PUPIL AT THE WINDOW: Now she's turning this way.

EDNA *(isolated at the front of the room, pointer drooping)*: Is it that Miss Starbody?

ANOTHER PUPIL AT THE WINDOW: Too far off to tell much, but—oh my stars, she's carrying switches in one hand and her head in the other.

(MAE *and* FAYE, *clinging to each other on their benches, scream.*)

WILLARD: That head would be the melon.
CECIL: She's coming this way.
JUSTIN: Saints preserve us! Look at her face!
CECIL: She's bound to be eighty!
WILLARD: But not a young eighty.

(*All the pupils at the window leap back to scramble onto the benches. EDNA hangs suspended at the front. All eyes turn to the door. Inexplicably, the school bell begins to toll as the door from outside begins to slowly open.*

At the door appears history's most fearful figure. She is all gray, black, and green from head to skirt tail. Pushed back from her straggle of gray hair is an out-of-date hood. Winking at her crepey throat is a metal brooch featuring a twist of human hair, in one of her clawlike hands is a bundle of switches; in the crook of her other arm, the effigy's melon head.

The pupils are frozen, except for MAE and FAYE, who fall off their benches. The fearful figure crosses to the desk, blotting out EDNA, and arranges switches and melon on the desk in full view.)

FIGURE (*in an awful, echoing voice*): I will have the melon for my noon dinner, as I do not have cooking privileges in my present lodging. The switches are for the rest of you, in the fullness of time.

(Without looking behind herself, she withdraws the pointer from EDNA's *hand and looks over the pupils.)*

FIGURE: I am Miss Delilah Dollop. You may call me Miss Dollop if you are called upon to speak at all.
CECIL: She ain't Miss Starbody.

(He ducks down as MISS DOLLOP's *sweeping gaze falls on him.)*

MISS DOLLOP: You, boy, did I call on you to speak?
CECIL *(in terror)*: No, ma'am.
WILLARD *(aside to* CECIL): At least she doesn't know who you are yet.
MISS DOLLOP *(to* CECIL): You, boy. Are you a Soper?
CECIL *(grabbing his head in more horror)*: Yes. Ma'am.
MISS DOLLOP: Yes, all you Sopers were alike: weedy, witless, and two straws short of a bale.
CECILIA *(rising)*: I'M a Soper. On both my mama's and my papa's side.
MISS DOLLOP: So I see. Sopers never know when to keep still, never did.

*(*CECILIA *wilts.)*

MISS DOLLOP: As even the slowest of you will discern, I am not Miss Starbody. Miss Starbody has been . . . delayed.
JUSTIN *(worried)*: Will she be long?
MISS DOLLOP: It will seem long to you. Meanwhile, I am the teacher, and like all the best teachers, I'm composed

chiefly of watch spring, whalebone, and dynamite. Do nothing to set me off, as for the time being I am your substitute teach—

EDNA (*barely visible behind* MISS DOLLOP *and clearing her throat*): Actually, I'm the substitute teacher, as I'm the oldest pupil, by far the smartest, and my daddy—

MISS DOLLOP (*whirling around*): You, girl, what are you doing up here? Get on your bench with the rest of them. Who do you think you are?

EDNA (*in a smallish voice, but holding her ground*): Edna.

(MISS DOLLOP *examines* EDNA *more closely, and* EDNA *pulls back.*)

PUPIL'S VOICE: Yeww, there are moths and things flying out of Miss Dollop's clothes.

MISS DOLLOP (*to* EDNA): If I recall correctly, I went to this school with your grandma. A big girl with a big mouth? Married one of the Wilberforces?

EDNA (*shrugging*): That'd be Grandma.

MISS DOLLOP: I knew your grandpa Wilberforce too, before he ran off with—

EDNA: That'd be Grandpa.

MISS DOLLOP: Take a pew. The only job you have here is to learn.

(EDNA *flops onto a bench as* MISS DOLLOP *takes up her post at the teacher's desk. Her gaze grazes Justin's shiny apple. She takes it up and holds it out in the manner of the Evil Queen in "Snow White."*)

MISS DOLLOP (*addressing the apple in a commanding voice*): Worms, come forth!

(*The pupils gape.*)

CECIL (*after a rapt pause*): By golly, look at that. The worms is crawling out of that apple. One's winding itself around the stem.

WILLARD: How'd she do that? Hey, Miss Dollop, how'd you do that?

MISS DOLLOP: I am fuller of worms than this apple. (*to apple*) You, the third worm, come out. I know you're in there.

Worms get wiggling, be gone, by gosh;

Find another McIntosh.

(*The pupils' collective gaze follows the invisible worms crawling out of the apple, dropping down on the desk, across the blotter, down to the floor, out the door. MISS DOLLOP throws the empty apple to JUSTIN, who has to catch it. He then ducks down, trying to be his smallest. MISS DOLLOP takes up the pointer, fingers its tip, and looks over the pupils.*)

MISS DOLLOP: Unless there's somebody else present who needs a worming, let's see if anybody in this school has any knowledge on any particular subject, other than running your mouths and making mischief. Who, for example, can spell the name of the president of these United States?

WILLARD (*still shaken by the worms, but pointing to the top of* JUSTIN's head): This squirt can, probably.

MISS DOLLOP: Then, boy, stand and deliver.

(JUSTIN *cautiously rises, holding the apple behind him, and clears his throat.*)

JUSTIN: Capital W-i-l-l-i—

MISS DOLLOP (*tapping the desk lightly with pointer*): Wrong. Sit.

EDNA (*to nearest other pupil*): He never got as far as "William." I'D have let him spell the whole name.

MISS DOLLOP (*who has the excellent hearing of all teachers*): He got the wrong man. I saw William McKinley early this morning, and I can assure you he's no longer the president of the United States.

EDNA (*behind her hand*): Why, the poor old soul! She's nuttier than a fruitcake. The president's in the White House, and she's here in the sticks. She's seeing things. They ought to put her in the Home for Decayed Teachers and hang her behind a door.

MISS DOLLOP: To continue this civics lesson: In the absence of the former president of the United States, who becomes president?

JUSTIN (*cautiously*): The vice president?

MISS DOLLOP: You're brighter than you look. And the vice president's name?

JUSTIN: Capital T-h-e-o—

MISS DOLLOP: Just say it.

JUSTIN: Theodore Roosevelt.

(MISS DOLLOP *nods approvingly.*)

EDNA (*in a carrying whisper to everybody*): Honestly, the woman doesn't know who the president is. We had better play along with her, in case she gets violent with those switches. She'll be seeing Abraham Lincoln in the outhouse next.

MISS DOLLOP (*above it all*): And now for long division.

CECIL: Long division! What is this, high school?

WILLARD (*sadly*): I'll never get out of sixth grade.

EDNA: Long division! Honestly! What's it *for*?

(*The scene dims once again as the pupils bend to their work under the direction of long-fingered, hollow-eyed* MISS DOLLOP.)

WILLARD (*rising and speaking to audience*): We put in a long morning under Miss Dollop. It seemed like several mornings. She handed out a year's worth of Fs in the first hour. And she'd mark you absent if your mind wandered. And my land, she was hard to look at.

But we learned us some long division, whether we wanted to or not. And whether we were in first grade or having another try at sixth. And I don't remember recess. We toed the line. We were too busy not to.

(*The room brightens to find* MISS DOLLOP *looking up*

from her bent pupils. The sound of a jingling harness comes from outside. Two or three pupils make to rise and run to the window.)

MISS DOLLOP: Sit.

(She crosses to the window herself, drawing her stained raiment around herself. Looking out, she fingers her brooch.)

MISS DOLLOP: Ah. Company coming.

(MISS DOLLOP resumes her post, this time in front of the teacher's desk.)

MISS DOLLOP: It would appear that I shall soon no longer be needed in this schoolroom. What a pity. Just when we were getting acquainted.

(The pupils stare as she gathers up the melon.)

MISS DOLLOP: Though I've recognized your faces from your families, I have not put a name to every face. Edna Wilberforce, be good enough to come forth to assist me.

(EDNA rises officiously and switches her skirt tails as she walks to the front of the room.)

MISS DOLLOP: Fetch me the roll book from that desk drawer.

(Without thinking, EDNA swerves around the teacher's desk. Though WILLARD, CECIL, and JUSTIN all wave frantically at her, she jerks open the drawer, and out bust all the frogs again.)

EDNA *(screaming and falling back)*: Oh no! How could I fall for that! Those repulsive frogs! Oh, the slime! And I think I stepped on one. It's all over my shoe.

(The pupils rise in a body, meaning to recapture the frogs.)

MISS DOLLOP: Sit.

(Everybody falls back. EDNA continues to writhe.)

MISS DOLLOP: Frogs—depart.
   Back to the underbrush, back to the bog;
   Back to the weeds and under a log.

(The pupils' collective gaze follows the invisible, hopping frogs around the desk, across the floor, out the door.)

CECIL *(to WILLARD)*: How in tarnation does she *do* that?

(MISS DOLLOP is by the door now. At the sound of stamping feet and voices outside, she pulls open the door, concealing herself behind it. In surge several parents, carrying a well-dressed, semiconscious young lady.

Covered by this crowd, MISS DOLLOP *exits with the melon.)*

ONE OF THE PARENTS (*a large, commanding woman in a large, commanding hat*): Boys and girls keep calm! Help is at hand!

EDNA: Oh no, it's Mama.

(The other parents place the young lady on a chair, where they attend her as she revives.)

WILLARD (*to* CECIL *and* JUSTIN): That'd be Miss Naomi Starbody unless I miss my guess.

MRS. WILBERFORCE (*fussing*): Oh, my dear children! Tragedy has been but barely averted. Miss Starbody was not discovered till nearly noon, underneath her upturned buggy in the gully under Hog Chute Bridge! And her runaway horse was found two fields away, grazing!

EDNA (*fingering her chin thoughtfully*): Never mind, Mama. We were quite all right on our own. Being the smartest, I myself took up the duty of being substitute teacher.

MRS. WILBERFORCE: Ah, my good, responsible girl, and always so modest. How much you remind me of myself at your age!

EDNA (*murmuring*): And Grandma.

(Beside them the lovely new teacher, MISS STARBODY, *stirs, rises, pulls the pins from her hat.)*

MISS STARBODY (*to nobody in particular, but addressing the world*): My pointer, please!

(*The scene dims as* MISS STARBODY *assumes her post, with pupils settled and onlookers looking on.* WILLARD *steps out to address the audience.*)

WILLARD: And this is the sum and substance of the first day of Miss Starbody's teaching career. She clung to her post a good many years, seeing me through the sixth grade at last and every one of us through the eighth. Though she was a young thing, direct from the normal school, she was a good teacher, and we let her. After all, the worms were out of the apple, and the frogs were out of the desk, and the effigy in the outhouse was nothing but strewn straw and rags, like an out-of-work scarecrow. And after what we'd been through, Miss Starbody looked pretty durn good to us. That particular first day of school turned out to be a moment in history. Though we didn't hear the news till later, the president of the United States, William McKinley, had died that morning. And so by the time school took up, the president of those forty-five United States was in fact Theodore Roosevelt. He began his administration on the same day as Miss Starbody began hers.

So that pretty well wraps up the first day of school in that year of 1901.

(*The scene behind the narrator brightens to find the stage empty of all except* CECIL *and* JUSTIN, *in caps, tramping in the open air with gunnysacks on their backs. WILLARD joins them.)*

WILLARD (*to the audience*): We lived in fear for some while that Miss Dollop would return as substitute teacher. We were forever asking Miss Starbody about her health and trying to keep her out of drafts. Still, as it turned out, Miss Dollop was never very far away. Us boys, me and Cecil and Justin, came across her one day after the first frost, when we were out hickory nutting.

JUSTIN (*whining*): I'm tired of hickory nutting, and my feet are fixing to drop off.

WILLARD: I said right along you were too young to come.

CECIL: And I got a burr in my boot. Let's rest a minute.

WILLARD: Let's get out of the graveyard first.

CECIL: Let's not. This boot's got to come off.

(CECIL leans against a solid object to pull off his boot.)

WILLARD: And don't lean on a tombstone. It don't show respect.

CECIL: It ain't anybody we know, is it?

(The three hunker to read the tombstone.)

WILLARD (*quoting*): "Miss Delilah Dollop, born 1799, schoolmistress of this district, faithful to the last."

JUSTIN (*continuing the quote*): "Died at her desk—Rest in Peace. Spelling Counts."

CECIL (*concluding the quote*): "Served out her final semester in the year of 1876."

(*All three boys freeze, stare at one another, then slowly turn toward the audience, eyes round with horror. The lights dim.*)

WILLARD (*to audience*): Come to find out Miss Dollop had been dead for right at twenty-five years that morning she floated out of the graveyard, through the outhouse and effigy, to substitute at Panhandle Ridge School. But that's a teacher for you. Show her a classroom full of kids and a pointer, and she'll move heaven and earth to get there.

And so we headed on home that afternoon, me and Cecil and Justin, toting our hickory nuts, never looking back in case something was gaining on us, hurrying right along as the shades of evening fell.

Blackout.

Production Note for *Effigy in the Outhouse*

Since this is a schoolroom story, any classroom will do, furnished with the basics in the stage direction: the blackboards and teacher's desk before as many benches (or desks) as the cast of characters requires.

A squeaking door and offstage bell to announce Miss Dollop's entrance.

A melon and an apple—real or artificial—are needed, but the frogs are invisible.

—R. P.

NOT SEEING
IS BELIEVING

by AVI

CHARACTERS

JULIAN .... Twelve-year-old boy
RUBY .... Eleven-year-old girl
MOTHER .... Mid-thirties
VOICE .... Can be male or female
FATHER .... Mid-thirties

Lights up on a children's bedroom. Two twin beds, parallel, a space between, with feet of beds toward audience. Between the beds is a window. In front of the window a chair. To either side of the window is a curtain that can be pulled across. On walls, at least two pictures. Against wall is a bookshelf, partially filled with books. A clothing closet with door. A bureau with drawers.

(*A boy—JULIAN—and a girl—RUBY—in pajamas, are sitting up in their separate beds. JULIAN is twelve. RUBY is eleven. Seated in the chair, between them, is their MOTHER. As the play begins, she is discovered holding a book, reading it aloud to the children. JULIAN and RUBY look bored.*)

MOTHER: . . . and so with the evil monster dead, the handsome and brave prince returned to the ancient castle and married the king's beautiful daughter, and they all lived happily ever after. The end. (*She shuts the book. Pause.*) Well, what do you think?

JULIAN: No offense, Mom, but it was pretty dull.

RUBY: Dumb, actually.

MOTHER: Oh, I don't know. I rather liked it.

RUBY: Ma, things like that don't *happen*.

MOTHER: Well, of course you're not meant to think it's really true. You're just supposed to see it in your mind's eye. Not even your real eye. It takes imagination to see what's . . . not there. I used to love stories like that when I was a girl.

RUBY: Kids don't see things like that now.

MOTHER: Try hard and you can.

RUBY: Mom, you can't see what's *not* there!

JULIAN: I just think you have to be old to like a story like that. No way can I see that happening.

MOTHER: Oh, well. *I* enjoyed it. And we'll start something new tomorrow night. Whatever you choose. Or maybe you can dream up a better story.

JULIAN: Like what?

RUBY: Duh! She can't tell you what to see in your dreams!

JULIAN: She can make a suggestion.

MOTHER: Okay, kiddos, no arguments. Now, you can talk some, but it's already past bedtime. Ruby, you have an early soccer game. Julian, you have Little League practice. In the afternoon we're going to Aunt Sue's. So time for you guys to get some sleep. I'll get the curtain. (*She gets up and draws the curtain over the window.*)

RUBY: Where's Dad?

MOTHER: Had to work late. He'll come in when he gets home. But you'll probably be asleep. (*She kisses the children one after the other.*) Good night, love. Good night, love.

RUBY: Night, Mom!

JULIAN: Night, Mom!

(MOTHER *goes, dimming lights. Children remain in bed. Pause.* RUBY *sits up.*)

RUBY: That story was REALLY pathetic.

(JULIAN *sits up.*)

JULIAN: She liked it. But I guess if she's going to read to
us every night—and you like that, don't you?
RUBY: Yeah.
JULIAN: Then it's only fair that she likes some of what she
reads.
RUBY: This one was hard to keep my eyes open for.
(*Yawns.*) Night.
JULIAN: Night. . . .

(*They settle down. Quiet. After a moment, the closet door
rattles. RUBY makes no movement. JULIAN shifts in his
bed but pays no notice. The closet door rattles again,
louder. JULIAN sits up.*)

JULIAN: What are you doing?
RUBY: Trying to sleep.
JULIAN: Then you are the *noisiest* sleeper . . .

(JULIAN *drops down. Quiet. Closet door rattles.*)

RUBY: Look who's talking. . . . Shhh!

(*Pause.*)

VOICE FROM CLOSET: You going to let me out?
JULIAN: What?

VOICE: You going to let me out of here?

RUBY (*sitting up. To* JULIAN): Will you *please* stop talking!

JULIAN: I'm NOT talking.

RUBY: You are too! (*Plops down.*)

(*More noise from closet.*)

JULIAN: Admit it! You were making the noise!

RUBY (*yells*): Wasn't!

(*Quiet. Closet door rattles.*)

VOICE: Are you going to let me out or not?

(JULIAN *sits up. Looks at* RUBY. *No reaction from her. He looks at closet.*)

VOICE: How many times do I have to ask? Get me out of here!

JULIAN (*to* RUBY, *whispering*): Ruby . . .

RUBY (*lying in bed, her back to* JULIAN): What?

JULIAN: I think . . . there's someone . . . in the closet.

RUBY: Julian, tell your dream to go back to sleep.

JULIAN: No, really. Sit up. Listen.

VOICE: Hey! I need to get out!

(RUBY *pops up. She looks at* JULIAN.)

JULIAN (*whispering*): See what I mean?

RUBY: How can I see what you mean when it's too dark to see anything? Who was that?

VOICE: And how many times do I have to ask? Let me out of here!

JULIAN: (*points to closet*): It's coming from in there.

(*Closet door rattles.*)

VOICE: I'm getting *very* frustrated!

RUBY: Julian . . . there's someone . . .

JULIAN: *Now* do you see what . . . ?

RUBY (*whispers*): I'm not sure I want to see. (*She gets out of bed.*)

JULIAN: Where you going?

RUBY: I'm going to get Mom. (*She starts to go.*)

VOICE: I didn't say get anyone! I said, get ME out of here!

(*RUBY freezes. JULIAN jumps out of bed away from closet.*)

VOICE: Didn't you hear me?

JULIAN: Who . . . who are you?

VOICE: If you opened the door, you could find out.

(*Kids look at each other. RUBY shakes her head. Starts to exit. At that moment the whole closet door falls open with a crash. RUBY halts. JULIAN stands by RUBY. They stare at closet. Pause.*)

JULIAN (*to closet*): Are you there?

VOICE: Of course I'm here.

RUBY: Then . . . come out.

VOICE: Can't.

JULIAN: Why?

VOICE: Your mother is coming.

JULIAN: She is?

VOICE: And she's not happy.

(The kids leap back into their beds and pretend to be asleep. MOTHER enters. Turns on light.)

MOTHER: Hey, guys. What's all the racket? You're sup-posed to be asleep.

JULIAN: We *are* asleep.

MOTHER: It doesn't look that way. Now, please quiet down and get some sleep. Night.

JULIAN: Night.

RUBY: Night.

(MOTHER turns off light. Leaves. Quiet.)

JULIAN *(sitting up)*: She didn't notice the closet.

RUBY *(sitting up)*: You could have told her.

JULIAN *(to the closet)*: You still here?

VOICE: Unless my eyes deceive me, it looks like I am.

JULIAN: How'd you know our mom was coming?

VOICE: Could see her in my mind's eye.

RUBY: How about letting us see you?

VOICE: I'm standing right here.

JULIAN: Where?

VOICE: HERE!

(RUBY *gets up and turns on the light. Looks around.*)

RUBY: If you're here, where are you?
VOICE: In your bed.

(RUBY *rushes to bed, throws back blanket.*)

RUBY: You are not!
VOICE: That's because now I'm sitting on the bookcase.
JULIAN (*still in bed*): How'd you get there?
VOICE: How do you think? I walked!
RUBY: What I want to know is how come we can't see you?
VOICE: I haven't the slightest idea.
JULIAN: Are you . . . invisible?
VOICE: I can see you.
RUBY: Just because you're invisible, doesn't mean we are.
JULIAN: Yeah, what do I look like?
VOICE (*describes actor*): Satisfied?
JULIAN: Can you describe yourself?
VOICE: Sure. I'm about one foot tall. Small head with blue
  hair. My orange eyes bulge. My hands are enormous.
  But my feet are very small.
RUBY: Gross!
VOICE: Sorry, it's what I am.
RUBY: Where do you come from?
VOICE: What's the first letter of imagination?
RUBY: I!
VOICE: Well, you see with an eye, right?
JULIAN: No, seriously, where do you come from?
VOICE: Doesn't matter where I came from—I'm here.

JULIAN: Then how come we can't see you?

VOICE: Maybe you don't spell your imagination with an eye.

RUBY: Very funny! Are you still sitting on the bookcase?

VOICE: No.

JULIAN: Where are you now?

VOICE: Under your bed.

RUBY: Why?

VOICE: Your father just got home. He's rushing up to say good night.

(RUBY *runs to light, turns it off. Kids jump back into their beds.* FATHER *enters tentatively.*)

FATHER (*whispering*): Anyone still awake?

RUBY (*after a moment*): I am.

(FATHER *goes to* RUBY's *bed, sits on it.*)

FATHER: Sorry I'm so late. Got held up. Have a good day?

RUBY: Okay.

FATHER: See anything interesting?

RUBY: The most interesting thing I saw was . . . like . . . invisible.

FATHER: I like that. Julian asleep?

RUBY: I guess.

VOICE: He is not!

FATHER (*turning*): Julian? You up?

VOICE: He's pretending to be asleep.

(*Puzzled,* FATHER *stands up, looks around.*)

FATHER: Hey, Julian, didn't know you could do weird voices.

(JULIAN *sits up.*)

JULIAN: Did I fool you?
FATHER: Absolutely. Anyway, I just wanted to say good night. (*to* RUBY) Soccer tomorrow? Who do you play?
RUBY: South Creek Ravens.
FATHER (*to* JULIAN): And you've got Little League?
JULIAN: Practice my knuckleball.
FATHER: Full day. Okay, guys, see you in the morning. Night!
JULIAN: Night.
RUBY: Night.

(FATHER *goes. Pause.*)

JULIAN: That closet thing gone?
VOICE: I'm still here.
RUBY: Where are you now?
VOICE: In the bureau. Top drawer.
JULIAN: You are not!

(*Bureau drawer slides out, falls.* JULIAN *comes out of bed. Looks.*)

JULIAN: No you're not.
VOICE: That's because I'm over here now.
JULIAN: Where's here?

VOICE: In your bed.

JULIAN: Get out!

VOICE: You could show a dollop of kindness.

JULIAN: Out!

VOICE: If you insist.

RUBY: Do you—whoever you are—have a name?

VOICE: Too hard for you to pronounce.

RUBY: Spell it.

VOICE: I don't know your alphabet.

JULIAN: You never told us where you come from.

VOICE: There's an old saying: On a clear day you can see forever. But I don't think you can see that far.

JULIAN: Fine. Then how did you get here?

VOICE: Don't know, actually. Just—there I was—in your closet.

RUBY: How come you came?

VOICE: Not sure about that either.

RUBY: Do you know what? I don't believe you. I mean, you don't have a name, you don't know where you came from, and you don't know what you're doing here. I don't think you really exist.

VOICE: Of course I exist!

JULIAN: PROVE IT!

(*Pause.*)

RUBY: Well?

(*The chair between the beds rises into the air and hovers there. The next moment it falls to the floor with a crash.*)

VOICE: Do you believe in me now?

RUBY: That was just a trick.

JULIAN: Ruby! Stop encouraging him! Maybe I should get Mom.

VOICE: She's already coming.

(The kids rush for their beds, cover themselves with blankets. MOTHER looks in. Lights come up.)

MOTHER: *What* is going on here?

RUBY: Nothing.

MOTHER: Did *nothing* make that racket?

JULIAN: Actually, yes.

MOTHER: I suppose the chair did it by itself.

RUBY: Honest, I didn't see anyone do it.

(MOTHER straightens chair.)

MOTHER: Were you having an argument?

RUBY: Sort of.

MOTHER: About what?

JULIAN: We were seeing things differently.

MOTHER: Okay. Fun is fun. But you guys REALLY need to get some sleep. It's way past your bedtime. Okay?

RUBY: Okay.

MOTHER: Night.

RUBY: Night.

JULIAN: Night.

(MOTHER starts out.)

VOICE: Good night from me too, old lady.

(MOTHER *halts.*)

MOTHER: What did you say?

JULIAN: Mom, it's nothing!

MOTHER: Julian, that wasn't very nice. I'd like you to apologize.

VOICE: Sorry!

MOTHER: Please, no more fooling around. You *must* get to sleep. Big day tomorrow.

JULIAN: We will.

RUBY and JULIAN: Night!

VOICE: Night.

(MOTHER *hesitates, looks around, then goes.*)

JULIAN: Hey, you! You're a troublemaker if I ever saw one.

RUBY: The trouble is we can't see him.

VOICE: I'm right here.

RUBY: Where?

(*Some books fall out of case.*)

RUBY: Okay. Just tell us. What are you?

VOICE: I told you, I'm not sure you have a word for me. But I've been thinking over your questions—you know, who, what, where, and why—and the thought came to me that maybe you're responsible for all of that.

JULIAN: Us?

VOICE: The both of you.

RUBY: How come?

VOICE: Maybe I'm here to prove—well—that I'm here.

RUBY: That's stupid.

JULIAN: Look, as far as I'm concerned, if I can't see you, you're not here.

VOICE: But I AM here.

RUBY: Not to us, you're not!

VOICE: To me I am!

JULIAN: Are you saying that NOT seeing is believing?

VOICE: Look, can you see China?

JULIAN: No.

VOICE: Well? Is China there?

RUBY: China's there, but all you are is a bad dream, or a bad joke, or some stink-o TV show without a TV.

JULIAN: I bet you're a homeless panhandler.

VOICE: I'm not asking for anything.

JULIAN: You do and be what you want. This is too weird for me. I'm going to sleep! (*He gets into bed, lies down, and pulls the blanket over his head.*)

VOICE: Your brother is not very polite to guests.

RUBY: You're not exactly a guest. I mean, you invited yourself.

VOICE: How can I prove to you that I exist?

RUBY: You could start by stopping being invisible. For example: Let me see you.

VOICE: Which? Start or stop?

RUBY: That's it! You're NOT here. I'm going to sleep too.

VOICE: Wait!

RUBY: Why?

VOICE: I thought of a way you could see me.

RUBY: How?

VOICE: If you were invisible—maybe two invisibles make one visible.

RUBY: Is that true?

VOICE: Worth a try.

RUBY: You're not trying to hoodwink me?

VOICE: I swear on a stack of . . . invisible Bibles.

RUBY: Could you really make me invisible?

VOICE: I'll have to see what I can do.

RUBY: Where are you now?

VOICE: Sitting on the chair, thinking. Okay! I know what to do. These curtains. Step behind them.

RUBY: Why?

VOICE: When you get behind the curtains, I won't be able to see you. You'll be invisible, right? Then you'll see me.

(JULIAN *sits up.*)

JULIAN: That's the dumbest thing I've heard all night. Standing behind a curtain won't make her INVISIBLE.

VOICE: You won't be able to see her, will you?

JULIAN: What about China?

VOICE: Just try it.

RUBY: This is SO stupid. But maybe it'll make him go away.

JULIAN: Be careful!

(RUBY *steps behind the curtain so that she can't be seen.*)

VOICE: Ready?

RUBY: Yup.

VOICE: Okay, then. Bang! There! You're—invisible.

JULIAN: She is not!

VOICE: Can you see her?

JULIAN: Look! I'll show you! (*He jumps out of bed. Yanks back the curtain.* RUBY *is not there. Pause.*) Ruby! Where are you?

RUBY'S VOICE (*from across the room*): Right here. Oh, wow! That thing is exactly what he said he looked like. You are so weird!

VOICE: There you are: Seeing is believing!

JULIAN: Ruby! Would you stop playing games! Where are you hiding?

RUBY'S VOICE: I'm right over here.

JULIAN: You are not!

RUBY'S VOICE: Am too.

JULIAN: Prove it.

(*Pause. A picture on the wall falls down.*)

RUBY: See?

JULIAN: I saw the picture fall, but I can't picture you!

VOICE: Hey, guys. Your father's coming.

(JULIAN *hurries into bed.* FATHER *comes into room.*)

FATHER: WHAT is going on here?

JULIAN: More than meets the eye.

FATHER: I'll say! Where's Ruby?

JULIAN: Ah . . . she went to the bathroom.

FATHER: Fine. But seriously, Julian. It's WAY past your bedtime. You guys *must* go to sleep. Mom and I are tired. We're going to bed. So no more. Please try to see things our way.

JULIAN: I'd be happy to see anything, Dad. Really.

FATHER: All right, then. Good night! When Ruby gets back, please see to it that you tell her what I said. (*Turns to go.*)

RUBY'S VOICE: How can I see what you said?

(FATHER *stops.*)

FATHER: Ruby, are you hiding?

JULIAN: Don't bother to look for her. She's invisible.

FATHER: Not funny, Julian. Ruby, I really don't care if you're invisible or not. Just pay attention to what I said and go to sleep. I'm getting annoyed.

RUBY'S VOICE: I can see that.

(FATHER *hesitates, then starts to go.*)

VOICE: And I can see you too.

(FATHER *again hesitates.*)

FATHER: Julian, this fake voice business is not amusing.

JULIAN (*to* FATHER): Don't look at me.

FATHER: Who else should I look at?

RUBY'S VOICE: Me.

FATHER (*to* JULIAN): What did you say?

JULIAN: Dad, trust me, we're never going to see eye-to-eye about this.

FATHER: I'm not asking you to see it my way. Just go to sleep!

JULIAN: Night.

(FATHER *goes.*)

JULIAN: See what you did? You're getting us into big trouble.

RUBY'S VOICE: Who you talking to?

JULIAN: Both of you.

RUBY'S VOICE: Sorry.

JULIAN: Anyway, it's not fair. I'd like to see this . . . thing too.

VOICE: Just become invisible.

JULIAN: How?

RUBY'S VOICE: Go behind the curtain. He'll make it happen.

JULIAN: What's it feel like? You know, becoming invisible. Does it hurt?

RUBY'S VOICE: Ever sit in the lunchroom and no one comes to sit down with you?

JULIAN: Yeah.

RUBY'S VOICE: Same as being invisible.

JULIAN: Okay. I'll try. (*He goes behind the curtain.*)

RUBY'S VOICE: Go on, make him invisible.

VOICE: I'm trying.

(*Pause.*)

VOICE: Okay! All done!

RUBY'S VOICE: Julian? You there? You okay?

JULIAN'S VOICE: I'm fine.

RUBY'S VOICE: I'm going to pull back the curtain.

JULIAN'S VOICE: Go ahead.

(The curtain pulls apart. JULIAN is gone.)

JULIAN'S VOICE: What's the big deal?

RUBY'S VOICE: Look around.

JULIAN'S VOICE: Oh, cool. You're right. He is weird.

VOICE: I told you: Seeing is believing.

JULIAN'S VOICE: I thought you said not believing is seeing.

VOICE: Same thing, isn't it?

RUBY'S VOICE: Wait a minute! If we can all see one another, we're not invisible—I mean, not to one another. Just others.

JULIAN'S VOICE: And since no one else is here, we're visible.

RUBY'S VOICE: But if they were here, we'd be invisible.

JULIAN'S VOICE: But if they were here, we might not see them.

RUBY'S VOICE: Like the lunchroom.

JULIAN: What about Mom and Dad?

VOICE: Parents never see their kids the way they see themselves.

RUBY'S VOICE: I think lots of parents don't notice their kids at all.

JULIAN'S VOICE: Actually, I think it's more that kids don't notice their parents.
VOICE: Let's try it.
RUBY'S VOICE: How?
JULIAN'S VOICE: The chair seems to get them.
RUBY'S VOICE: Let's do it.

(Pause. The chair rises and falls. Pause.)

VOICE: Good job! Here they come.
JULIAN'S VOICE: Which one?
VOICE: Both.
RUBY'S VOICE: Oh my God! This I gotta see.

(Enter MOTHER and FATHER.)

MOTHER: Ruby! Julian! This simply has got to stop!
FATHER: You're acting like two-year-olds.

(Pause.)

MOTHER: Where are you?
BOTH KIDS: In bed.
MOTHER: Oh, stop it! I want you to come out from wherever you're hiding.
JULIAN: Actually, I am in bed. Ruby isn't.
MOTHER: Where is she?

(Another picture falls off wall.)

FATHER: Kids, if this goes on any longer, we're going to have to seek out some suitable punishment. Last warning! Both of you, now, into bed. Fast!

RUBY'S VOICE: We *really truly* are in bed. Both of us. Now.

MOTHER: How am I supposed to believe you if I can't see you?

JULIAN'S VOICE: Can you see China?

FATHER: Julian, stop this nonsense! I'm getting angry. Wherever you are, look at me. I don't know where you're hiding, but your mother and I are going to leave this room for one minute. Just *one* minute. When we come back, we expect to *see* you in your beds.

MOTHER: Is that perfectly clear?

FATHER: Show us you can be trusted.

BOTH KIDS: We'll try.

(The parents go out.)

RUBY'S VOICE: Hey, you! Make us visible again.

JULIAN'S VOICE: Fast.

VOICE: Not sure I know how.

RUBY'S VOICE: But I don't want to be invisible anymore.

VOICE: Might help in your soccer game.

JULIAN'S VOICE: Wicked. What about me?

VOICE: You'll be able to steal every base on the diamond!

JULIAN'S VOICE: That would be cheating. I'm going behind the curtain.

VOICE: Wait a minute!

JULIAN'S VOICE: What?

VOICE: Have I convinced you?

RUBY'S VOICE: About what?

VOICE: That "seeing is believing" is no different from "not seeing is believing."

JULIAN'S VOICE: What about "believing is seeing"?

VOICE: Actually, that's the best way of all.

JULIAN'S VOICE: Great. All in favor say "eye!"

VOICE: The eyes have it!

RUBY'S VOICE: Will you guys stop! They are about to come back. I'm going back behind the curtain. Make something happen.

VOICE: How about—not believing is not seeing.

JULIAN'S VOICE: Just make me visible.

(Curtain shakes. Pause. Curtain opens. JULIAN is there.)

RUBY'S VOICE: Well?

JULIAN: I must be visible. I can't see you.

RUBY'S VOICE: My turn.

JULIAN: Hold it!

RUBY'S VOICE: Now what?

JULIAN: We've got to make him promise to go away.

RUBY: Do you?

VOICE: I'm afraid we're not seeing things the same way.

JULIAN: If you don't go, we're going to get into a sea of trouble.

VOICE: Very funny! But I can see your point.

JULIAN: At least we're all seeing the same thing at last.

RUBY'S VOICE: Guys! I'm going behind the curtain.

(Curtain shakes. Pause. Curtain opens. JULIAN *pulls curtain.* RUBY *is there.)*

RUBY: Have I changed any?

JULIAN: Not as far as I can see.

RUBY *(looks around)*: Where did HE go?

VOICE: I'm in the closet.

RUBY: Really? *(Looks.)* I don't see him.

VOICE: Remember? Not seeing is believing.

JULIAN: Do you promise not to come back?

VOICE: I'll see what I can do.

RUBY: I think it would be better to make yourself not seen!

VOICE: See you around!

JULIAN *(to* RUBY): Let's get the closet door up.

(They put door back into place.)

RUBY: Are you in there?

(No response.)

JULIAN: Guess he left.

RUBY: Dad's coming!

(They rush to their beds and get under the covers. FATHER *opens door, looks in.)*

FATHER: Much better. Thanks. Now have a good night's sleep, guys.

JULIAN: Night.

RUBY: Night.

(Pause.)

RUBY: Julian?
JULIAN: What?
RUBY: Do you believe any of what happened?
JULIAN: Sort of like being on a seesaw.
RUBY: Not funny! Night.
JULIAN: Night.

(The kids lie down. Pause. The chair rises, hovers.)

VOICE: Did you hear the one about the blind carpenter?
RUBY: What about him?
VOICE: He picked up his hammer and saw.

(Chair falls.)

Blackout.

Production Note for
Not Seeing Is Believing

The voices can be projected from behind the set of the room. It's suggested that the actors move around so their voices come from different places.

While it's not necessary, this play could be even more effectively produced by putting a number of small speakers around the set, so as to suggest voices coming from a variety of places.

The rising chair can be achieved by attaching a very thin but strong fishing line to the chair and then threading it through an overhead pulley, which can be manipulated backstage.

The kids' disappearance should be made through a hole in the set behind the window curtain.

The production would be helped if the actor providing the Voice had a very distinctive tone.

—Avi

★ WHO'S WHO IN THE CAST ★

AVI chose the word "hoodwink" because it is a combination of two very ancient words and combines the notions of hiding, seeing, and teasing into one word—which could be a summary of what his play is about. He is the author of the Newbery Medal winner *Crispin: The Cross of Lead*. He is the author of more than sixty books for children and young adults. He has received two Newbery Honors and many other awards for his fiction. He lives with his family in Denver, Colorado. Visit him on the Web at www.avi-writer.com.

SUSAN COOPER chose the word "dollop" because it sounds so wonderful and has always been one of her favorite words. She is the author of the Newbery Medal winner *The Grey King* and the Newbery Honor book *The Dark Is Rising*, both part of her bestselling Dark Is Rising sequence. She lives on an island on a saltmarsh in Massachusetts, and her website is www.thelostland.com.

SHARON CREECH chose the word "raven" because she just loves the word. It not only conjures up that spooky black talking bird in Poe's poem, but also black, inky colors and dark night and eerie things. She is the author of the Newbery Medal winner *Walk Two Moons* and the Newbery Honor book *The Wanderer.* She is also the author of several bestselling novels and picture books, including *Love That Dog* and *Heartbeat.* She lives in New York with her husband. You can visit her online at www.sharoncreech.com.

PATRICIA MacLACHLAN chose the word "knuckleball" because it has always seemed to carry with it great mystery. It's a quirky pitch as well as a quirky word, and that appeals to her. She is the author of the Newbery Medal winner *Sarah, Plain and Tall.* She is the author of many well-loved novels and picture books, including *Journey*, *Baby*, and *Edward's Eyes.* She lives in western Massachusetts.

KATHERINE PATERSON chose the word "panhandle" because she was at her wit's end. The deadline was drawing close and she had NO WORD. Desperately, she closed her eyes, opened up her desk dictionary, and stuck her finger onto the page. She opened her eyes to see that her finger had landed on the word. She was horrified, but what could she do but submit it? She is the author of Newbery Medal winners *Jacob I Have Loved* and *Bridge to Terabithia*. Ms. Paterson has received numerous awards for her writing, including National Book Awards for *The Master Puppeteer* and *The Great Gilly Hopkins*. She lives with her husband in Vermont. You can visit her at www.katherinepaterson.com.

RICHARD PECK's chosen word never made it into the collection. To expedite matters, he called in his word and left it on the voicemail of the editor. The word was "justice." The editor heard "Justin." Guess what the editor's name is? Mr. Peck is the author of the Newbery Medal winner *A Year Down Yonder* and the Newbery Honor Book *A Long Way From Chicago*. Peck has won a number of major awards for the body of his work, including the Margaret A. Edwards Award from *School Library Journal* and the National Council of Teachers of English/ALAN Award. He lives in New York City.